The Slaying
of the Dragon

THE SLAYING
OF THE DRAGON :
Tales of the Hindu Gods

retold by Rosalind Kerven
with a foreword by Prabhu Guptara

Illustrated by Meena Jamil

ANDRE DEUTSCH

First published in 1987 by
André Deutsch Limited
105–106 Great Russell Street, London WC1B 3LJ

British Library Cataloguing in Publication Data

Kerven, Rosalind
   The slaying of the dragon and other tales
   of the Hindu gods.
   I. Title   II. Jamil, Meena
   823'.914[J]   PZ8.1

   ISBN 0–233–98037–7

Phototypeset by
David John Services Limited, Maidenhead, Berks

Printed in Great Britain by
St Edmundsbury Press, Bury St Edmunds, Suffolk

Contents

Foreword

Prabhu Guptara

When I was growing up as a boy in India, I had a storyteller of my own – our cook. He used to tell us wonderful stories throughout the day. There was no shortage of stories with him, and if he couldn't think of one sort of story he could always think of another.

Once, my fingers accidentally touched the flames on which he was cooking, and my hand felt hot and stingy. I think it must have been the very first time he allowed me to help with the cooking. He grabbed my hand and gently hit my ear with my burnt finger. He made up a story on the spot to explain what had happened. A genie lived in each of my ears, he told me, and if I touched one of my ears as soon as my fingers felt stung, then the genie would make me well.

It worked too. But he said that the kind of genie who lives in the ears isn't very strong. The genie who lives in water is much stronger. So if my fingers got too stingy, it was better to put them straight into cold running water from the tap. Whether you touched your ear or put your fingers under water, you had to do it quickly, or the genie's power wouldn't work.

Even in those days, I didn't quite know whether to believe him or not. But I still touch my ear or put my hand under tap water if my fingers get burnt when I am cooking.

Stories are powerful things. They take you into new worlds, full of new sights and sounds and smells and feelings. In these new worlds, things may be done quite differently from the way they are done at home or in school. People in story worlds may value and believe in different things from you. But you can live in that different world as long as the story lasts. You learn a lot, and enjoy yourself too.

That is why, in the old days, rich people rewarded good storytellers with valuable presents. Those who were poor didn't need to give anything to storytellers, because they were often excellent storytellers themselves. In those days, stories were told and jokes were cracked every evening, in every single Indian home. And in every Indian village and slum, people still sit together and tell each other stories. Some stories are from their own ordinary lives, all twisted and blown up to make them more amusing for listeners. Some stories have been passed on many times. There are stories from history, there are stories about animals, and there are stories of our gods and goddesses.

In addition to my cook, who told us stories during the day, I had another storyteller for bedtime. My father used to read me stories from books, or sometimes make them up. But we really couldn't go to sleep without listening to a story from my mother.

Mainly my mother's stories were about Indian gods and goddesses, such as are included in this collection. Many of them my mother would tell us again and again. I particularly enjoyed stories like *The Princess and the Ten-Headed Demon*, a tale of Rama's nobleness and *The Boy Who Moved the Mountain*, which is full of Krishna's mischievousness. These are known to every Indian child, even if that child is from a family that follows Islam, Buddhism, Christianity, or some other religion. Some stories come from God, some come from human minds, some come from demons. At least, that is what Indians have always believed. Some stories which come from God or from demons get twisted by our own minds as we retell them. That doesn't mean they are any less enjoyable. They may even be more enjoyable.

Did they really happen? To real people? Many Indians believe that these stories are true. Other Indians believe that they are false. They value the stories, they say, because they help us to understand how we should live.

There is no way of proving if the stories in this book are true. You can decide for yourself if they teach you anything about being brave, or honest, or strong. But I tell these stories to my own children whenever I can, and they will tell you that stories of Indian gods and heroes are good to listen to – and good to read. You may or may not believe the tales. You may or may not learn anything from them. But you will, at least, enjoy them.

The Fish with the Golden Horn

Oh the wickedness! Oh the sin! The folly and filth and evil! Whatever was the world coming to?

Beggars and invalids lay moaning in the streets, while those who had good fortune shrugged and hurried past. Half the people frittered their time away idly drinking, the rest gambled and argued and fought. Some whipped their children, others kicked their animals. They scattered poisons into the rivers, and rubbish all over the land.

But everyone knew that something was wrong.

"All the suffering that goes on!" they said, "doesn't it make you want to weep?"

And: "There's children starving, old folks lying ill for want of a doctor, whole families living amongst the rats. Something ought to be done!"

But nothing was done, for no one would do it. Instead, the poor got poorer, the sick got sicker and the land shrivelled up with neglect.

At that time, the gods looked down onto the Earth. They saw that the world was full of decay and sorrow, and knew that the End had almost come.

However, there was one man who was not in the least bit wicked, and he was a king called Manu. Whenever he could escape from his dreary kingly duties, he spent a lot of time thinking; and the more he thought about it, the more certain he became that a king's life was not for him.

So one day, Manu called the Crown Prince to him.

"Son," he said, "I've decided to give up the throne. I've had enough of politics and trouble. From tomorrow, you shall be king. I'm going to become a hermit."

The next morning, true as his word, King Manu kissed his wife goodbye, threw all his bejewelled royal robes into a disgusted heap and went walking off into the mountains. He took nothing with him except for the simple clothes he stood up in, a staff to help him along the more difficult paths, and a small wooden bowl in which to beg for a few mouthfuls of rice.

Well, he wandered far and even further, until at last he reached a cave. It was right up in the mountains by the shore of a small lake, and Manu thought it would do just nicely to keep him dry and warm. So there he decided to stay. He ate nothing but wild roots and berries and saw no one from one year to the next. But he was happy! He spent all his time strengthening and purifying his mind and body, watching the seasons turn, thinking and praying as hard as he could to the gods.

Before he said his prayers each morning, Manu always used to wash himself very carefully in the cold waters of the lake. One day, he was doing this as usual, when suddenly he felt something wriggling and tugging through his beard.

"Whatever can it be?" said he to himself.

His beard had grown so long and tangled with the years, that he had to prod his way carefully through it; but at last, what should he pull out of it but a tiny golden fish!

"Save me, save me!" cried the fish.

Manu blinked at it kindly.

"Save you, little brother?" he said. "Of course I will, though I can't imagine what you need me to save you from. I certainly won't eat you, if that's what you mean."

But the glistening, golden thing did not seem in the least bit comforted. Still it blinked anxiously up at him, whispering, "Save me, please, please!"

Manu scratched his matted, hairy head while he thought.

"How about this?" he said at last. "I could fill up my old wooden begging bowl with water and then you could swim about in that and stay close beside me in my cave."

At this, the fish seemed to look a little happier, so Manu did as he had suggested.

That night, he set the fish in its bowl on the rough floor next to the spot where he lay down. It felt very odd to have another living creature there beside him, after all his years of solitude. He tossed and turned and could not sleep, for the golden fish haunted his dreams.

Next morning, he turned at once to look at it in the bowl, to check that it was all right. And indeed it was, but goodness, how it had grown! When he had put it in there yesterday, there had been plenty of room for it to swim around in; but somehow, in the stillness of the night it had got so much bigger that now it was flopping out over the sides.

"Save me, save me!" gasped the fish.

Manu thought quickly, and remembered a large earthenware storage jar he had once made himself, that he kept at the back of his

7

cave. He ran at once to fetch it, then down to the lake to fill it with water. As soon as he got back, he carefully slid the fish inside.

For a few anxious seconds it hovered uncertainly, gulping down water; then suddenly it was fine again, swimming and diving about.

Manu went out into the early morning sunshine. He had his bath and tried to do his exercises; but today he just could not get them right. He tried his utmost to think quietly and to say his prayers, but his mind just would not stay still.

For the strangeness of that fish echoed through and through him. What was it? And what did it really want?

The next night was just as the last one. Manu went to bed on the floor of the cave with the fish stored safely beside him; and when he woke up next morning, the beautiful golden creature had grown so much that it could scarcely keep its gills under water.

"Save me, save me!" it cried.

"Oh dear, oh dear!" Poor, kindly Manu was doing his best, but it was not an easy task.

"Perhaps I should put you back into the lake?" he asked it nervously. "I'm sure you'll be quite safe there now – you've grown so big that none of the other fish would dare to eat you."

The fish seemed happy enough at that, so far as he could tell. So he picked it up in his trembling hands, and carried it, gently as a new-born babe, down to the clear blue waters.

The fish dived in and swam off, an enormous streak of gold.

Every so often, Manu pottered down to the shore of the lake and took a peep to see how the fish was getting on. Each time, it swam up to greet him; and each time Manu noticed two peculiar things. The first was, that whenever he looked into its eyes, they seemed somehow deeper and more mysterious than the very ocean, filled with a million swirling secrets. The second thing was, that by the day, by the hour, even by the minute, the fish continued to grow.

Manu found that he had a queer, excited feeling deep in the pit of his stomach. He knew now, beyond any doubt, that this was no ordinary creature. He began to devote every hour that he was awake to watching over it.

By and by, it grew so much that even the lake was too small to hold it. Now its scales glittered in the sunshine with polished, golden fire, reflecting up and over the towering mountains. And from the centre of its head, something else grew gleaming: a single golden horn.

It was king of the waters, invulnerable, magnificent; yet once again when it saw Manu waiting, it begged him, "Save me, save me!"

Whatever was he to do, now that it had outgrown even the lake? Manu decided there was only one thing for it: he must take it to a river – not to any river, but one that was very special and fit for the fish's glory: he would take it to the holy River Ganges.

Now the Ganges rose quite nearby in that very part of the mountains, and by means of careful seeking and exploration, Manu discovered that it could be reached from the lake through a complex network of mountain streams.

So he wove himself a rope of creepers and tied it carefully to the fish's golden horn; and with this he led it gently through the waterways and craggy hillsides and down bumpy, stony gulleys. His feet grew sore and his legs ached but his heart and mind were filled with concern for the fish; and at long last, they reached the sacred river.

Manu untied his rope and watched the fish streak off. But no sooner had it swum a little way, than it turned back and seemed to wait for him; and through the rushing waters he heard its plaintive cry:

"Stay with me, Manu, and save me!"

So Manu walked beside the fish as it swam slowly down the Ganges, growing bigger and still bigger by the day.

They passed out of the mountains and into the foothills; out of the foothills and into the plains. They passed villages, towns and magnificent cities. People left their drinking and gambling to stare in astonishment at the sight of the hermit and the fish with the golden horn. Yet they all turned away with hard-hearted laughter as soon as they heard it pleading:

"Save me, I beg you to save me!"

At last they reached that place where the river ends and flows out into the sea.

"I can help you no longer, dear friend and brother," said Manu, "for here is the great ocean itself. Surely there'll be enough room for you there, however much bigger you grow!"

The fish said nothing, but swam straight out into the foaming waters. The waves tossed it up and down, and the goldness of it swelled out and up, up and out, until it filled every corner to the horizon. Its horn grew and grew, straight, strong and gleaming until it reached the very heavens.

Now the fish seemed to fill not only the water but the whole Earth

– the whole of the Three Worlds! Manu watched it, full of wonder, more than a little afraid.

"Manu!" came its voice, and it was near and far and everywhere. "For many days and nights you have cared for me: you have given up your whole life to serve me. Can it really be that you do not know who I am?"

Manu tried to answer, but the words stuck in his throat. He did not dare . . . could the secret hope that had slowly risen inside him really be coming true? He felt bathed in an everlasting golden sunset. At last he whispered,

"You are . . . my lord? Lord Vishnu?"

"I am Vishnu indeed," said the fish.

"But why have you come to me? Amongst all my sins . . . my lord! How can I possibly deserve this?"

"Manu, listen," said the fish who was really Vishnu, the great god who protects all life. "I come not to reward you, but to give you a task. Soon the Three Worlds with all their wickedness must be destroyed, for the present Age is nearing its sorrowful end. This is how it has been destined since the wheel of Time began with all its thousand mysteries.

"I shall tell you what will happen. Lord Shiva will start his dance of destruction that brings first the fire and then the flood. The wicked ones will burn to ashes, and then they will drown in the waters.

"But you, Manu, will neither burn nor drown. With my protection, you will float like a leaf upon the chaos. I will protect you, and in your turn, you will protect the seeds of all things that live."

Manu fell in a tremble to his knees on the seashore, blinded by golden light.

"My lord, but how shall I do it? How shall I save the seeds of the living? I am so poor and unworthy!"

"Once you were a powerful king," the god reminded him. "Now you are a sage and have wisdom at your fingertips. Use your power and wisdom, Manu, to build a ship. It must be large and very strong. On it you must take two of every living creature, and the seeds of every flower and tree that grace the Earth. When the waters rise, I will be there to guide you. Doomsday is coming, but know this: from every End there grows a new Beginning. I promise you that a new Age will dawn and the Three Worlds will become whole again. Then people will sing your praises, for the great deed you were able to do."

The fish had melted away, but the god's presence was everywhere. Now there came an explosion of light like a million sparkling cinders, so brilliant that Manu screamed out loud.

He blinked, lifted his hands to shield his eyes; and when at last he dared to look again, the light had disappeared.

For a long, long time he sat very still, very silent on the sea-shore. Hours passed, then days. He forgot about thirst or hunger.

Was it really true? He had been chosen! Singled out and given such a task by the gods!

Manu knew that he must start right away. He gathered wood, made tools and nails, and began to build his ship.

All around him the world went on with its wickedness.

"Whatever are you getting up to, you silly old man?" people called to him. "Hey, stop wasting your time with all this working! Come and get drunk with us instead!"

But Manu simply shook his head and got on with banging in nails.

Then he went wandering around the Earth, through forests, deserts and mountains, calling in all the birds and animals, insects and reptiles, to take shelter on board his ship. Two by two by two they came. Next he wove himself a huge basket and collected in it the seeds of every single plant that he could find.

And still the drunken rabble stood by jeering.

At last, everything was ready. Manu sat, quiet and alone, to wait.

He stared at the sky. He could see the stars dancing. He fancied that when the sun set, it was bigger than it should be, and that its rays were scarred with blood   . . .

Blood and smoke! Death and fire! As he watched, now the stars, the moon and sun burned up and scattered across the sky. Heat and ashes! Manu shivered and looked around – to see a world engulfed by flames!

But a golden halo hovered around him, the ship he had built and all that sheltered within: the halo kept them safe.

Now the fire turned into thunderclouds, and the sky began to rain.

Water and hail, ice-grey, torrential! It thudded on land and sea, washed everything away. Cold, wet and bottomless, it swallowed the Earth and all things in it, until at last there was nothing left but ocean.

Safe inside his ship, Manu watched and waited as fire and flood rose all around.

By and by, beyond the edge of the End, he saw a light. It grew and drifted towards him until, within its glow he saw the wonderful golden fish.

"Come," said the fish. "I will lead you as you led me. Throw me a rope. Moor your ship to my horn. I will take you to where we are going. As you saved me, so I will save you. I will show you where the New Age begins."

Manu hesitated, but then a great snake came out from the depths of the ship where it had been sheltering. It wound its tail tightly around the ship's prow. Manu threw its head towards the fish. The snake caught it, and coiled its other end around the fish's golden horn.

Through the darkness, through the silence, through the End and the Beginning of everything, the golden fish swam. The fish pulled the snake. The snake pulled the ship and all its survivors, slowly towards the dawn.

There at last, the light rose clear and steady! There was the New Age bathed, like the fish, in gold.

From within the boat, Manu saw the Earth heaving, fresh and green, out of the waters. He heard the crystal call of bird song, the cry of a baby, the gentle lowing of cows.

He had come to journey's end.

Daughter of the Mountain

She was beautiful as all the flowers of spring and summer. She could dance as gracefully as fallen leaves tossed by the wind in autumn. She wore ornaments that sparkled like snow on the tree tops in winter. And she was madly in love with Lord Shiva.

Her name was Parvati, which means 'daughter of the mountain', for her father was Himalaya, lord of the tallest, mightiest range of mountain peaks in all the world. Graceful as she was, Parvati had also inherited her father's strength, for her devotion to Shiva was fierce and staunch as rock.

Surely even mighty Shiva must feel tempted to return the love of one whose brilliance lit the sky like Parvati's? Certainly the goddess herself believed so, and every day she tried dancing and smiling to entice him. But Shiva just ignored her, and did not even give her a glance.

Was it because he already had another wife or lover? No: the fact was that Shiva had lost all interest in women. He had given his heart to what he considered to be 'higher things'. All day and night he sat cross-legged on the lonely peak of Mount Kailas, deep in meditation, trying to fathom the innermost secrets of life. He did not bother to wash, nor to cut or comb his hair. He smeared his body with ashes and starved himself until the bones showed through his flesh. His finger nails grew long and dirty like the claws of a wild beast.

Yet still Parvati ached with love.

She was quite open about her feelings, and soon all the other gods heard about her distress. They could not help but feel sorry for her; and they were mystified by Shiva's lack of interest in a woman

13

blessed with such perfection. More than that: they agreed it was unnatural and dangerous for the great Destroyer to shun the company of women. So they decided to do what they could to help.

Now amongst them was one called Kama, the god of love and desire. The other gods persuaded him to go and seek out Shiva and to waken in him the spark of love.

So Kama went off and eyed the mighty one from behind the shelter of a rock. How mindless and still he sat there! – a perfect sitting target. Kama strung his bow with an arrow of sweetly scented flowers, then stood up and aimed his shot . . .

But at that very instant, Lord Shiva sensed the other's presence. Quicker than a spider's blink, he woke from his trance, whirled round and opened up the third eye in the middle of his forehead.

Kama realised what was about to happen, but a split second too late. From the Destroyer's eye, a flash of lightning leaped out, and zigzagged straight to the spot where the gentle love god stood. He tried to cry for mercy but there was no time: within an instant there was nothing left of him but a heap of smouldering ashes.

Shiva shrugged with a thin smile of regret, then went back to his meditation.

If it was hard luck on Kama, it was even worse for his wife, the goddess Pleasure. Oh, what bitter tears she cried over and over the wretched remains of his body!

While she was sitting there sobbing, Parvati came along. She saw Pleasure's tear-stained face and the heap of ashes; she gazed at Shiva sitting a little way off, lost in thought with his third eye blinking, and guessed at once what had happened.

It is all my fault, she thought to herself, *for poor Kama would never have been destroyed, had he not been trying to help me. I must do my best to make amends to his dear wife.*

So she went and sat by Pleasure, and hugged her kindly as if she were a younger sister. By and by the two unhappy women exchanged a vow of friendship, and each shared with the other her sorrow.

"Listen," said Parvati, "I will make a promise to you, Pleasure. When at last I succeed in winning Lord Shiva's love – and I shall, I *shall*, even if it takes me to the end of Time! Well, when he is mine, I swear I shall not give him one kiss until I have made him bring your Kama back to life again."

Pleasure dried her eyes as best she could.

"Parvati," she said, "if you were not the daughter of rocky

Himalaya, I would say such a promise were worthless; but I believe that you have enough strength and patience to do what you say you will. Thank you then, my sister – from the bottom of my heart!"

She got up and turned to walk away, pausing to call back, "Let us hope that next time we meet both your sorrow and mine will all have melted away!"

For a long time after that, Parvati sat staring across the peaks at her beloved Lord Shiva, wondering what she could do to turn his heart.

"One thing has become quite obvious," said she to herself, "he is certainly not influenced by beauty." She let out a sigh, like a summer's breeze. "So – I shall have to show him that I'm more than a pretty face!"

She pondered some more, while day turned to night and then to day again.

"I have it!" she exclaimed at last. "Don't they say that when mortal people on Earth want to win the love of their favourite god, they do it by showering him with devotion? Yes! They worship his image and make him offerings over and over until they receive an answer to their prayers. If it works for mere humans, surely it will also work for me?"

So Parvati set to work for many hours and days until her fingers were sore, carving a statue of fine white marble that was an exact likeness of Shiva. She set it up on a peak immediately opposite Mount Kailas where the god (if only he would look!) could not help but see it, and smothered it in garlands of flowers.

Then she brought delicate silver dishes brimming over with wine and milk, with honey, sugar and fruits, and placed them before the statue. She lit the finest incense to swathe it in sweet smelling smoke; she drew sacred patterns in jewelled colours to honour the ground at its feet.

All day long she knelt before it, singing Shiva's praises, worshipping his greatness, offering him her humble devotion and prayers.

Across the valley Lord Shiva sat, immobile as a marble statue himself. Did he see her, did he hear her? If so, he made no sign to show it. He was utterly lost in that ecstatic inner world known only to mystics and sages. What use could he possibly have for love?

But still the daughter of the mountain did not give up.

"Very well, my lord," she whispered, "if I cannot beat you at your game, I shall have to join you. I shall become a hermit too, I shall study the ancient wisdom and meditate on it until I am wise and holy, as you are. Then I shall meet you in that secret place where your heart has lost itself – and there, at last, you will have to give me your love!"

So she took a knife and cut off all the gleaming tresses of her thick black hair. She threw away her silken saris, her peacock feathers and her golden rings, her necklaces and bracelets and anklets, all sparkling with a thousand precious stones. She dressed in a thin wrap of rags and tatters, smeared ashes over her face and body, and went off into wild places alone.

She learned to twist herself into the most difficult postures of yoga until energy rushed through her body like a river in full flood. She learned to endure the heat of the midday sun, the cold of an ice-bound river, without feeling the slightest twinge of pain. She learned to make her mind utterly clean and light and empty; and in all that emptiness she found secret knowledge, more patience and even greater reserves of strength.

How many eternities had she been waiting for now? Parvati did not know; but suddenly she became aware that someone was watching her: a fat, rather ugly-looking priest.

"Greetings, goddess," he called.

From far, far away, Parvati slowly brought her mind back to the here and now. she untwisted her slender arms and legs, and bowed with folded palms to show respect to her visitor. But what an exceedingly sour-faced man he looked!

"Tell me," said the priest, with an unpleasant grin, "Whatever is one so lovely as you doing here all alone, tormenting yourself with such tortures?" He reached out a hand, making as if to steady her; under his clammy touch Parvati was cold and hard as stone.

"I do it to win the one I love, holy man," she said. "I have vowed to live the harsh life of a hermit-woman, and not to smile at any other man, until I have achieved my aim."

"I see, I see," cackled the priest. "And if it is no offence to ask you, goddess, what is the name of this wonderful man you are after?"

Parvati's black eyes shone.

"It is Lord Shiva," she answered softly.

The priest threw back his head and laughed out loud.

"Shiva?" he cried. "No! What, that revolting-looking madman who hasn't once washed himself for a thousand years? Surely not, goddess! Whyever should a woman as lovely as you waste your time chasing after the most despicable of all the gods?"

Parvati looked straight through him.

"Oh, I have heard all the unkind things that people say about him," she said. "But Shiva is the greatest god in the Three Worlds! He alone has power to destroy all things, and then to recreate them anew. He alone makes the mountains tremble and the sun explode; he is the mighty master of the eternal cosmic dance!"

"No doubt all that is true," said the priest. He leaned forward on his staff and fixed his mean eyes on Parvati's shining face. "But listen to this, my girl: your beloved Shiva is also the most foul mannered fellow that ever lived. Here's a few home truths to set you thinking.

"Firstly, he hasn't even got a home to call his own: when he's not lost to the world up here on his mountain, he's either staggering about in gutters or kicking his way through graveyards, or grabbling through the mud with his begging bowl. Secondly, he's not only dirty, but he has the most disgusting set of habits: he spits, he picks his nose, he goes everywhere carelessly scratching . . . "

"Enough!" cried Parvati. "I've heard quite enough from you. Please go away and leave me in peace!"

"Ah," said the priest, "but I haven't finished yet, my dear. You must let me tell you about his terrible temper and his murderous ways. It takes less than a fly's sneeze to annoy him. Say one wrong word, and he'll burn you up with a blast from his third eye." (Parvati could not help but remember poor Kama.) "Let two wrong words stir his anger and he'll start hurling firebrands about, here, there and everywhere, and even kick the king of the gods off his throne! I warn you, my dear, his rage burns hot enough to turn the whole universe to ashes! Then there's the unsavoury tastes that he has: skulls and snakes and . . . "

"Stop, stop, STOP!" Parvati screamed at him. "I refuse to listen to any more!"

She clapped her hands over her ears and closed her eyes tightly. "Just get out of here – quickly – go on!"

But the priest did not go. She felt his hands reach out to wrench her own away from her ears; she felt the intensity of his stare, willing her eyes to open.

"Leave me be!"

"That's a fine way to speak to the one who loves you."

She drew back in horror: was this nasty, ugly priest really daring to woo her? At last, she could not resist his will any more and was forced to look up and meet his gaze . . .

"*Oh!*"

The priest had gone.

In his place, Lord Shiva himself stood before her!

The great god held fast to her hand and drew her gently towards him. True, true, his hair was long and tangled: *like seaweed*, thought Parvati, *wild among the waves*. True, his skin was pale with dust and ashes: *ah*, she thought, *how brilliantly it shines with divine light!* True, too, that dangerous energy smouldered in every pore of his being: *the very flame of love and creation, of all that gives him life!*

A smile, wry yet tender, played about his mouth.

"So Parvati," he said, "you have won me in the end! No, not with your beauty, goddess, though I must admit that it's dazzling indeed. Nor with your worship and devotion, though I could hardly help feeling flattered. You have not even stirred my interest by the wisdom and self control you obtained through your years of living as a hermit, though I am willing to believe that you have learned more secrets and deeper ones than even I understand.

"Oh, daughter of the mountain, I will tell you the truth, why I cannot help but come to you. It is this: you have seen my light always, always, however much it lay hidden under the mist and filth of my thickest worldly disguises. For a hundred aeons you have stayed true to me: though I did everything to make you suffer and turn you away, always I have been your only love. In all the cosmos, there cannot be another woman whose heart is as strong and noble as yours is!

"Parvati, I have hurt you too much: now let me show you the strength of my love."

He leaned forward to kiss her. But Parvati's heart was indeed strong: she could not take a reward without first fulfilling that promise she had made long ago.

So she pushed him back with a teasing smile.

"Oh no, now *you* will have to learn to wait and to master a little patience! My love must be earned, too, you know."

Shiva stared at her, beginning to tremble with an attack of his famous rage. But a woman cannot fear the one she truly loves. Parvati stood firm before him and went on, "You see, I'm not the only innocent goddess who has suffered by you, my lord. I have an husband, all because of me. I made a solemn vow to Pleasure that I would make you bring him back to life before I ever took so much as a single kiss from you. Do this for me, my lord: prove you can raise the dead as well as destroy the living!"

Shiva's trembling grew greater and more fearsome . . . then burst into unexpected laughter.

"Oh, you have me trapped, my brave Parvati! You understand me too well: you know I am powerless to refuse anything that you ask of me, now that you have lit the flame of my love. Sweet lady, show me where the ashes of Pleasure's husband lie, and I will do what you want at once."

So Parvati took his hand and led him to the wretched spot where Pleasure still made a pilgrimage every day to weep. He opened up his third eye and this time sent the life-spark leaping out to the remains of the dead god's body.

At once Kama himself sprung up, whole and new again, and threw himself into his wife's delighted arms.

"So my love," said Shiva turning in all his glory to Parvati, "you have won my heart, and I have done for you what was asked. Only fools would hang about any longer! Come, let us go at once to see your father, mighty Himalaya, and tell him to arrange our wedding without delay!"

Thus at last Shiva and Parvati were united as husband and wife. It is said that the whole Universe leaped with joy at their first kiss!

The Churning of the
Sea of Milk

Fate swung in the balance as the eternal question echoed across the Universe: *Who is mightier, the gods or the demons?*

"By all the powers of good, it must be us!" cried Indra, King of the Gods, Lord of Storms and Thunder.

He had summonsed all the other gods to a meeting at his palace on the peaks of Mount Meru. There they sat, cross-legged, talking of blessings and evils, watching the day sink to sleep behind the clouds.

"But listen, my friends," Indra went on, lowering his voice and glancing nervously around lest a demon should be within earshot, "I believe I've been cursed. Just lately I've felt the most terrible weakness, as if all the strength were draining out of me."

Brahma stood up, stretching his four arms with a weary sigh. "I feel it too," said he. "My powers aren't what they should be. What is happening to us, friends? Unthinkable evil will creep into the Three Worlds unless we are strong enough to stand constant guard and throw it back. We must find a tonic, some medicine to heal our strength."

There was a long silence. Against the pink-and-golden evening sky, Vishnu's voice said softly, "We need Ambrosia."

"Ambrosia?" repeated Indra.

"The magic drink," said Vishnu, "the liquid of immortality. If only we could get hold of it, all our strength would return."

"In that case," cried Indra, "you must tell us, if you can, where this wonderful drink is hidden, Lord Vishnu, and the quickest way to get there."

"You know," said Vishnu, "that around the edge of the Earth lie seven oceans, one within the other, like rings. First is the ocean of salt water, then that of syrup, then wine, melted butter, milk, whey and, lastly, the one of fresh water.

"This is what I have heard: that the Ambrosia lies buried in the middle of the fifth ocean, at the heart of the Sea of Milk. But it is not easy to come by. To find it, that ocean must be churned up for many hours and days until it froths like cream. But I fear that with our present troubles, even all of us working together may not have enough strength to do this, though we are gods."

"Yet it sounds as if this Ambrosia is our only hope," said Indra. "We must find a way to get hold of it somehow!"

"There is a way," said Vishnu, "and that is – by asking the demons to help us."

At this, a great hubbub of protest arose amongst the gods:

"But that's impossible!"

"Never since Time began have we shared a task with the evil ones!"

"Suppose they try to cheat us out of it!"

"It is a risk indeed," agreed Vishnu, "yet it is part of the price we must pay, and I swear this to you: the risk would be well worth taking for just one sip of this miraculous drink! But more than this: you will find that within the Sea of Milk many other priceless treasures lay hidden. Believe me, when you see the marvels it yields, you'll laugh out loud at your own hesitation!"

The other gods pondered on this speech for a while, and talked about it amongst themselves. At last, Indra stood up and said, "It seems that your wisdom is always worth listening to, Lord Vishnu. We have agreed to do as you say."

So the gods went to the demons, and asked if they would help them in this task.

"Treasure?" replied the wicked ones, their eyes sparkling with greed. "A magic drink that brings immortality? Of course we'll help you, gods. We'll come along at once!"

In this way, the forces of good and evil united and travelled as far as the oceans which mark the Earth's end. They hastened straight across the salt water, the syrup, the wine and the melted butter; but when they came to the white shores of the Sea of Milk they stopped.

"Lord Vishnu, we have come to where you have led us," called the gods and demons with one voice. "Now tell us how we should begin to churn it."

Vishnu stood before them, smiling in all his glory. "Here is your churning stick," said he; and he showed them a pointed mountain towering eleven thousand leagues high, covered in vines and forests, tinkling with bird-song whenever it moved. "And this noble snake, whose name is Vasuki, shall be your rope."

Then, before their eyes, Vishnu suddenly turned himself into an enormous turtle with a broad, thick shell.

"Now," he commanded, "balance the mountain on my back, for I shall be its pivot and bear all its weight as you churn it."

With much huffing, puffing and heaving, Indra and the other gods lifted the mountain onto his shell; then the turtle dived with it into the milky ocean, down to the bottom of the waves.

Vasuki the snake swam after it, twisting and twining round and round the mountain peaks, tightening himself like a cord. Then the gods lined up on one side and took hold of one end of the serpent, the demons seized the other end, and soon they fell into a rhythm of pushing Vasuki to and pulling him fro until the mountain began to twitch, then to turn and spin.

Fast, then faster ever faster, they churned. The mountain whirled round, and the Sea of Milk became veiled by a spray of creamy foam. The gods grunted and the demons groaned; and all the while, Vasuki the snake grew hotter and hotter like a tinder-stick rubbed by flint – until all of a sudden, the breath belched out of him in a cloud of smoke and flames!

Asss! It set fire to the sky with flashes of lightning. *Haagh!* It sent streams of steaming, molten lava splashing up from the Earth. The mountain roared in agony and the Sea of Milk screamed.

Now the gods and demons were blinded by effort, heat and madness.

"Help us!" they shrieked, "Mercy, mercy! We shall all burn away to ashes!"

But in all the Universe, there was nothing and no one who could possibly help, beyond their own selves . . .

With the last of his strength, Indra untangled his fingers from the snake. Somehow, he struggled his way up to Heaven, where he knew his ranks of storm clouds were waiting. For who else should make relief from heat and burning but he, the mighty Thunderer, bringer of rain? With trembling hands, he unleashed the clouds from their

tethering, pierced them with thunderbolts and then, over the terrible fire of mountain and ocean, he let their waters gush down.

Ah, how wet and cold and soothing! The rain met the flames with an explosive hiss of steam; it smothered the smoke and blanked out the lightning. It calmed the sickening waves and the sweating, heaving mountain; it extinguished the deadly fire in the breath of the snake.

The gods and demons fell back, each to their own side, weak with relief. "Give us more strength, Lord Vishnu," they panted, "or we simply cannot go on."

Below the Sea of Milk and the mountain, enshrined in the body of the turtle, like the rock at the Universe's heart, Vishnu heard them calling. He sucked the strength out of his own eternal being and wished it into the gods and demons above.

His power seeped into their bodies, it sank into their minds. They knew it like a rushing of waters, like a voice that whispered, *Don't give up, the magic is almost completed, if only you will keep on churning.* So the gods and demons fell to work again, heaving and rocking with snake and mountain . . .

. . . Until at last, at last, treasures beyond the wildest dreams of Heaven began to spill forth.

First the Moon was born, and then the Sun; then the goddess Lakshmi, a wife for Vishnu, bringing good fortune to the Three Worlds. Next came a magic horse, a four-tusked, snowy elephant, a sparkling jewel and the glowing goddess of wine.

For a few moments the miracles were lost in a veil of poison that sent the gods coughing and staggering in another agony of fear; but the Lord Shiva danced out from their midst, protected by magic chanting, and swallowed the poison away.

Now the good things came again. There was a tree of paradise, heady with the flowers of granted wishes; and after it a sacred, milk-white cow, fat with the fruits of desire.

And then – and then –

A stately figure stepped from the cream of the ocean. He carried a cup that was full and sweet to the brim.

"I am Dhanvantari!" cried he. "Physician and magician, chemist and alchemist – I bring you what you long for. Strength and power, energy, immortality – Ambrosia, the magic elixir of life!"

The gods dropped the snake and the demons dropped the snake. They stood staring at the vision of Dhanvantari, so that for a few moments of eternity, the whole cosmos seemed to hold its breath.

The stillness was broken by a gross roar from the demons:

"By darkness and evil, the Ambrosia shall be ours!"

"Haven't we earned it with our sweat and tears?"

"What have the gods offered us so far of the presents that the Sea of Milk has given forth?"

"Nothing, nothing!"

"Seize it, brothers: let's swig it all up before the gods can get a taste for themselves!"

With that, the demons all threw themselves at Dhanvantari, and wrenched the brimming cup from his hands.

Off they raced with it, leaping over the four inner oceans, entering the Earth, and slipping down to the shadowy underworld regions where wicked things love to dwell.

The gods stared after them, numb with shock. What an end to the efforts that had weakened them more than ever: to have the magic drink, the only thing that could save them, snatched from under their eyes. Oh, what disaster and misery would come now to the Three Worlds?

Under the ocean, Lord Vishnu shrugged off the shape of a turtle. He rose through the waves and came to the other gods.

"Shame on you," he cried. "Do you think we can't outwit the villains? Listen, you know that I have as many shapes and forms as the sun has rays. I have a plan that is sure to melt them into easy defeat and this is it: I shall turn myself into a woman!"

And there, indeed, where just now Lord Vishnu had been, a woman stood smiling, more beautiful even than Lakshmi, with the enchantment of love in her eyes.

The gods let out a gasp of admiration; but in that instant, she was gone – running off on the demons' trail, leaping over the four inner oceans, entering the Earth and slipping down to the shadowy underworld regions where wicked things love to dwell.

There, in the dark, dank passages and caverns, the demons smelt her perfume and saw the light of her coming; each was trapped in a spell of desire as one by one they turned to stare. They forgot their longing for a sip of Ambrosia, overcome by the pain of love.

"Oh pretty thing!"

"Wonderful lady!"

They crowded round to admire her.

"Let us be your servants!"

"Tell us what we must do to win you!"

"Oh, you can have my love for a simple price," said the enchantress who was really Vishnu. "This is it: give me that cup of liquid that you guard so carefully between you and let me take it where I want to."

"Take it, yes, yes, take it!" cried the demons, for they were breathless at her beauty. "But perfect lady, we beg this of you: wherever you go with it, let us also follow."

"You may follow after me certainly," smiled the enchantress. She held out her slender hand and, tenderly, passionately, the demons placed the cup of Ambrosia into it.

"Come then, if you want to," said she; and carrying the magic drink, she led them back through the Earth and across the oceans, to where the other gods still waited on the shores of the Sea of Milk.

"Lady, lady, what will you do now with our wonderful potion?" asked the spellbound demons.

"I shall give a sip to all those who truly love me," she answered.

At this, the demons were still more delighted – for who could possibly love her more sincerely than they?

But as they watched, their delight quickly turned to anger. The enchantress passed the magic drink along the waiting line of gods. Each one drank long and deeply, though the cup stayed brimming full. When she reached the end of their row, she did not offer the cup to the demons: instead, she threw them a last posy of mocking laughter – then turned herself back into Vishnu!

The demons were beside themselves with fury. They pounded into a ferocious war dance and shrieked filthy, blasphemous insults at the gods.

". . . And as for you, high and mighty Vishnu, you're a scheming cheat and a trickster!"

"But you played the first trick," said Vishnu calmly, "when you tried to steal the Ambrosia. It is a primal law of the cosmos that every deed, good or bad, shall come back to you. It is only natural, is it not, that we gods should pay you back?"

"Give us the Ambrosia!" the demons yelled, ignoring him.

"Let us taste it, let us have the share that we've earned!"

"Didn't we work as hard as you at the churning? Aren't our own muscles stretched and aching, our hands torn to ribbons and our backs bent low with the pulling?"

"Give it to us, we command you – let us have that part of the

Ambrosia that rightly belongs to us!"

"NO!" roared Vishnu. "What would become of the Three Worlds if the demons were given the gift of living for ever? How much would the wheel of Time have to spin before the gods could ever triumph again?"

"Then we will fight you for it!" shrieked the demons; and without further warning, they took up arms and threw themselves into a battle that shook the Universe from end to end.

Screams and curses, brute strength and weapons: never had the Three Worlds known such horror, never had the demons' anger been so great!

But the gods alone had drunk the magic potion. Now their goodness would thrive for ever; they could never be destroyed.

And so at the last, when the Sun itself was stained with spilled blood and Mother Earth was weak and moaning, a shower of arrows tipped with gold shot down from Heaven, straight to the hearts of the demons.

"It is our end!" they screamed. "Evil has lost its hold for another Age, we must give way to the gods immortal . . . "

Then down, down they sank, weakened in their wretchedness, to the depths of the seven seas.

"So," said Indra into the silent emptiness that was left, "we have our Ambrosia, our strength and immortality. Once more, we have won the balance."

Vishnu nodded his head with a weary but satisfied smile.

"Here," said Indra, handing him the still brimming cup of Ambrosia. "Take this, my lord. You told us how to find it and you won it back for us when it was stolen. Truly, you are our protector, Vishnu! It is right that you should take care of it for all the gods."

Vishnu held the potion reverently in his hands.

"In Heaven's name," he promised, "I will keep our strength safe in it for ever."

The Dwarf's Footsteps

There was once a king called Bali who was clever, cunning and strong. He ruled well and carefully from his royal palace, and always remembered to serve the gods. But Bali had one terrible fault: he was greedy. He wanted more than was good for him. He wanted his kingdom – and thus his power – to grow and keep on growing.

Why should he want more when he already had so much? No one could say. Nevertheless, there were rumours. People whispered that his greed was part of a greater wickedness that Bali kept carefully hidden. It was even murmured – behind closed doors, when none of the royal spies were near – it was murmured that Bali was not a man at all – but a demon!

Of course, no one could quite be sure. To all intents and purposes Bali looked like a normal man. There was nothing outwardly demonic about him. Moreover, he was fair and decent to all the people who worked for him; he made public show of saying his prayers every day; he dropped gold coins into the bowls of beggars; and he paid his respects to the priests.

And yet . . . and yet . . . how had his kingdom grown so big, so quickly? What persuaded rival kings and neighbouring princes always to give in and sign their land away into his keeping? How did he manage to win every single battle he ever fought? What sort of magic lay behind his extraordinary power?

None of these questions could ever find an answer; but meanwhile King Bali's power grew and grew.

Soon he ruled the whole Earth; but that was not enough.

A little later he took over the Sky as well. Still Bali was not satisfied.

And then, at last, he won control of the Heavens.
Now he was Lord of the Universe, master of all creation!
How he wallowed in the praises and adoration of his subjects:
"Hail to mighty Bali, King of the Three Worlds!"

One day when Bali was sitting in his palace, feeling pleased with himself as usual, one of his servants came hurrying in.

"Oh Mighty King," cried the servant, almost tripping over himself as he swept the ground with a bow, "oh Greatest Majesty that ever lived, oh . . . "

"Yes, yes?"

"Your Majesty, one of your subjects is outside and humbly begs the favour of seeing you."

King Bali stroked his triple chin.

"And what sort of a person is it who wishes to bathe in my glory?"

"Your Majesty, he is a dwarf."

"A dwarf!" exclaimed the king angrily. "How dare a mean, creeping dwarf expect me to dirty my presence with him? Go back at once and tell him . . . "

"But, Sire," interrupted the servant, very very politely, "this dwarf is also a priest."

"Hmm. A priest?" Now, although King Bali was not afraid of anything, he treasured his power so greatly that there were one or two things he was always rather careful about. In particular, he was wary of priests. It didn't pay to take risks with them, or to offend them. For if they decided to take revenge . . . well. Priests, of course, had direct contact with the gods. And powerful as he was, even the mighty Bali did not fancy an argument with them.

"Go back and tell this, er, priest," said he, "that I shall be absolutely delighted to see him."

"Yes, your majesty." The servant backed away, as humbly as he had come.

Very soon he was back again followed by a curiously shrunken man. He stood no taller than Bali's waist, had a very long beard, and was wearing the simple robe of the holy orders.

"Come here, my good man!" called Bali. "Take a seat. That's right. Now, what can I do for you?" He grinned slyly behind his whiskers. "A priest's wish, you know, is always my command."

The dwarf hauled himself up into a chair next to the king's throne. Small he might be, yet he was very quick and agile. Good looking too. His skin almost seemed to glow (perhaps in reflection of his holiness?) with a curious bluish sheen. His eyes were deep and very bright.

"Your Majesty," he said, "forgive me for asking such a foolish question, but we priests are so busy that we can't always keep up with events. Is it true what they tell me? Are you really lord and master of the whole Universe?"

Bali tried, without success, to look modest.

"Well, only because you ask so frankly . . . my dear chap, I've never been one to boast about my achievements . . . but the fact is that yes, indeed I am."

The dwarf-priest smiled.

"In that case, oh glorious King, I hope you may be able to grant me a small request?"

"Haven't I already said?" Bali was getting impatient. "Just tell me quickly whatever you want and it shall be yours!"

"It's just a little something for myself you see," said the dwarf. "What I want is a piece of land.

"But of course," said the king, enjoying this chance to show off his generosity. How much do you want?"

The dwarf fixed him with his bright eyes.

"I like to think," he said, "that over the years my priestly life has helped me to gather wisdom, and a wise man never asks for more than he really needs. So what I want from you, King Bali, is just this: as much land as I can cover in three of my own strides."

Bali looked down at the dwarf's funny, stubby legs. He didn't like to laugh at the afflicted, of course, but – well! He stifled a chuckle by pretending to cough. Three dwarf strides indeed! Why, that was less than an ant's share of his mighty kingdom!

"I say," he cried, "are you really sure that's all you want? So little . . . "

"I shall ask for nothing more," the dwarf-priest answered, "so long as you give me your solemn royal promise that these three strides' worth of land shall be mine as soon as I have measured them."

"I promise," said King Bali promptly. He knew that a promise to a priest was not to be made lightly, for if it were broken the gods would regard it as a terrible sin. But such a small, such a silly request . . . whatever did he have to lose?

"Bali," said the dwarf softly, "your promise is made. Now you shall see what you have done!"

He stood up. Then all at once he began to grow.

Bit by bit, his limbs flowed out like water from a spring. They stretched, elongated, grew tall, strong, enormous. He was not a dwarf any longer – suddenly he was a giant!

King Bali cried out in terror:

"Fool, oh fool that I am! Who is this? What madness have I promised to give him?"

The dwarf-giant, the blue-skinned priest towered over him, laughing.

"Ho, Bali, don't you make offerings to me daily? I can scarcely believe that you don't know me! You who sing my praises so loudly in public: surely you are not afraid when I come to show my face?"

"Vishnu!" screamed Bali, "It's you, oh my god, the great Lord Vishnu! Oh great one, magnificent one . . . why have you come to me?"

"I have come," replied Vishnu, "to seize the Universe back from you, you demonical old rascal! Did you really think that you could cheat the gods out of Heaven for ever, eh? Well, let us see what you have promised me. Here is my first stride – so!"

Through his fear and trembling, Bali gaped and saw the blue-skinned god step across the whole width of the Earth.

"One world is mine already!" said Vishnu. "Now my second stride is . . . so!"

This time it was the Sky he stepped across.

Bali hung his head and wailed.

"Two worlds!" cried Vishnu. "Now, you must watch this, Bali, don't try to hide! And so – my third stride!"

He stepped across the Heavens.

"Three worlds in three strides," he said. "You have promised me all this, Bali – the whole Universe shall be mine! What have you got to say to that, your majesty? Look at me: I haven't asked for more than you can give me, have I? Answer me, you miserable, mighty king!"

"My lord," whimpered Bali, "good Lord Vishnu, take it all! The Universe is yours! It always has been! Only a greedy fool like me could ever imagine that it was possible to steal it from the gods."

He met Vishnu's eyes, and saw kindness shining from them behind the angry scorn.

"So tell me, Bali," said the blue-skinned god, "tell me – now that your reign is finished, what shall I do with you?"

For one who has tried to out-do the gods," whispered Bali, "there is only one possible punishment, and that is to go to hell."

Vishnu nodded, but his face clouded with sadness.

"That is true, Bali – and yet, demon that you are, you have not been thoroughly a bad king. How can I soften this punishment?"

"Oh my lord," said Bali hoarsely, "let me humbly beg just one favour of you. Let it be your own foot that sends me down to those terrible underworld regions – one of those noble feet that won the whole Universe back for the gods!"

"So it shall be," said Vishnu, "and beyond this, Bali, I shall not pass further judgement. I shall leave you there, out of harm's way, bound up in cords beside all your cronies. One day your turn will come to be reborn again. What will your next life hold for you? Let those who hear your story decide for themselves whether you deserve it to be thoroughly miserable; or if you have earned yourself at least a tiny morsel of good."

The Tears of Death

Long ago in a forgotten Beginning, Brahma created all things that live. There were birds and animals, fish and insects, reptiles and human beings. He was delighted by all their different shapes, sounds, smells and habits, and loved to watch them scurrying busily and self importantly across all the corners of the Earth.

However, there was one problem that Brahma had not thought of: once he had made all these creatures, there was nothing he could do to stop their numbers from growing. For in this Golden Age, love was everywhere. Birds built nests and raised large clutches of fledglings. Cubs and kittens were born in twos, in fours and sixes to the animals he had clothed in fur. And year by year humans took to marrying and to producing enormous families of children.

Brahma began to worry. All these creatures were multiplying so fast, they were over-running Mother Earth!

"Help me, for I am sinking!" that goddess began to complain to him. "All these creatures are so heavy, they are pushing me down, down into the waters. My rivers and oceans are chock-a-block with fish. There's scarcely room in my treetops for another bird to roost. My forests are overflowing with beasts, my plains are teeming with things that creep and run. But worst of all, human people are growing so fast in cleverness, skill and numbers that soon they will wear out every inch of my land. Grandfather, I beg you to think of a remedy before it is too late!"

"Yes, yes, I promise I shall save you," said the Creator; but secretly to himself he muttered, "Oh, fool that I am, I should have foreseen that this would happen!"

He peered gloomily down from Heaven, and even in that moment saw another hundred-thousand living things hatch from their shells or slip from their mothers' wombs.

"By the sacred mysteries, I shall have to put an end to this before it gets totally out of hand! Yet how am I going to stop it? I seem to have given these beings unlimited powers to keep making more and more likenesses of their selves!"

He watched the Earth a little longer.

"There's only one thing for it," he sighed, "I shall have to get rid of them."

So Brahma breathed in and then he breathed out, until from the mouths and nostrils of his four heads great coils of fire burst forth. He harnessed them to a bow like flaming arrows, and got ready to shoot them towards the creatures that live on Earth.

"STOP!" roared a mighty voice.

Brahma whirled round, and at once all the fiery arrows were extinguished. There before him stood Lord Shiva, pale as ashes, still as the eye of a storm.

"What by Heaven are you doing, Grandfather?" Shiva asked him softly.

Brahma looked embarrassed.

"I'm trying to remedy the mess I've got things into down there on Earth, that's all," he said. "I've made far too many living beings, you see. There's only one solution, Shiva: they must all be destroyed."

Shiva looked down at the Earth. He saw the colours of birds' wings and butterflies, smiled at the sight of women and dragonflies dancing in the dappled sunlight, watched tigers and deer as they ran with the grace of the wind.

"Grandfather," he said, "how can you bear to bring an end to such beauty – especially when you have created it all yourself?"

Brahma shook his heads sadly.

"I can see by one glance," Shiva went on, "that this dreadful task you have set yourself racks you with grief. So I beg you to grant me a boon."

"What do you wish for, Lord Shiva?"

"I wish for this," said Shiva, "that all creatures on Earth who have to die may be born again. I do not ask that any should ever be immortal; only that they should have the gift of re-birth and life over and over for as long as the wheel of Time shall turn."

"I am happy to grant that for you," said Brahma.

THE TEARS OF DEATH

Shiva nodded with satisfaction, then turned away to go wandering off through the Heavens.

"Wait!" Brahma called after him, "I see one coming who perhaps can help us . . . "

"I know her well," Shiva called back over his shoulder. "Ask what you will of her, Grandfather, you do not need me. Her name is Death."

Then he was gone, and a young woman was standing there. Her slender limbs and finely carved face were dark as ebony, and she was dressed all in red. Rubies flashed round her throat, her arms and ankles, and in the black night of her hair.

"Dusky one!" exclaimed Brahma as he gazed at her, "Oh dark goddess! Does one so lovely as you really call herself Death?"

The goddess folded her palms and bowed before him.

"That is the name I was given when I was sent to you, Grandfather. I am told you have a task for me. I tremble to know what it is."

"Death," said Brahma, "the answer is a simple one, though it may not please you. You have been sent to destroy the creatures that I have made to live on Earth."

A great silence throbbed through the Heavens; then: "No!" she cried, "I shall not do it!"

She raised her ruby eyes to plead with the great Creator; they grew wide with horror, then melted into pools of tears.

"Oh, holy Grandfather, how can you ask such a thing of me, an innocent, tender woman? It is impossible!" The tears overflowed and ran in gushing rivers down her ebony cheeks. "I swear that I can't! Do you expect me to murder old men who have grown precious as the years have brought them wisdom? Or slaughter little children whose laughter fills the world like music? Do you think, in cold blood, that I could kill harmless fathers as they labour to make Earth rich and fruitful, or mothers that are like well-springs of comfort and love? Do you take me for a demon, Grandfather? Do you think I could bear to listen to the anguish of those you might let me spare, the ones who must watch their loved ones die? How could I ever stand the torture of their grief and curses?"

"Death," said Brahma shortly, "there is no argument, nor any escape. You have been sent to me solely to fulfil this bitter purpose. That is your destiny. It will be best if you undertake this task at once, without delay."

The young goddess bowed humbly before him, not daring to say any more.

"Go," said Brahma, "be on your way."

So Death went; but not to Earth, nor did she look for any weapons which she could use to destroy creatures.

Instead she crept to the loneliest place she could find on a craggy peak in the mountains; and there she stood, balanced painfully on one leg while the wind and rain lashed round her, calling: "Grandfather, I'm going to wait here like this forever, without moving or flinching, until you release me completely from this cruel task!"

Brahma watched her unhappily. He said nothing, he did nothing. A hundred years passed. Ten thousand years passed. Fifteen million years passed. Still the dark goddess did not move. At last Brahma could bear her discomfort no longer.

"Foolish woman!" he called. "Stop torturing yourself! Go kill the beings on Earth as I have commanded you!"

But Death did not obey him.

"Grandfather, " she answered hoarsely, "I can see I must go to even greater lengths to prove the sorrow that your command has brought me. Now I vow that I shall starve myself, eating nothing but air until you promise to change your mind."

Another twenty thousand years went by. In her scarlet robes, the ebony skinned woman was slowly wasting away.

"This is madness!" exclaimed Brahma in exasperation. "You will not win me over by such deeds of self denial. Death, I command you yet again: go and fulfill your destiny!"

But Death did not obey him.

Instead, she found still rasher ways to make her protest. She crouched silent, without shivering, in torrents of icy water. She wandered far from shelter in a sun-baked wilderness, slept by the lairs of animals that were sharp in tooth and claw. She looked constantly for agonies that were ever more unspeakable, unthinkable, praying that by suffering herself, Brahma would release her from causing pain to any creature on Earth.

At last, after countless ages and aeons had passed and gone, Brahma went and tried coaxing her with gentleness.

"Goddess," he said, "let me explain to you the order and nature of material things, for that may make it easier for you to carry your burden. You must understand that to die is good, for without its opposite, life itself cannot be. Besides, I have promised Lord Shiva himself that all who die will be re-born again. What greater gift could I give my creatures? When the old grow weary, it will be a welcome release for them to make room for the young. When leaves decay, they feed new shoots on the tree. So it shall be from one Age to the next. Worlds may come and go and come again, but the Triple Universe in its essence goes on for ever."

Death relaxed. She slipped slowly from the agony of her tortures.

"Oh, Grandfather, " she whispered, "I have tried my utmost to change your mind, through millions and millions of years. What more can I do?"

"I can never be moved," replied Brahma, "though truly I am sorry. Death, please make your way to Earth now. You do not need to carry any weapons. I shall ease your task as much as I can – you will find you have fulfilled it without even trying, for destruction will be born from your own sorrow. I promise that no one will blame you. You may wander through the world wherever it pleases you; and weep as freely as you will."

So at last the goddess went down to Earth. She walked here and there, dark even against the shadows, bearing her sorrowful beauty like a pain. She kept carefully away from all living creatures and wept rivers of tears without end.

Brahma took pity on her, knowing that she could not bear to kill. He stole her tears and turned them into diseases, into wounds that fester, into the slow decay of old age.

Thus everywhere that Death went, everywhere she wept, sickness, injury and decay went too. Softly, silently, these things crept into the bodies of living creatures. Sometimes in peace, sometimes moaning, sometimes in anger, one by one they began to die.

And Death herself passed each one by, neither seen nor seeing, crying bitterly for the sadness that she could not help but bring.

The Boy Who Moved
a Mountain

In all the village of Gokula, there was not a more mischievous lad than Krishna!

Who untied the cattle and let them loose in the meadows? Who stole the honey-and-almond sweets that were cooling in the shade of a doorway? Who chipped a hole in the pot and leaked the yoghurt that was curdling? Who even (oh shame on the boy!) made that puddle of pee on the floor?

All the other children knew who to blame at once:

"It was Krishna, Krishna, Krishna!"

"Him, son of Nanda, son of the village headman!"

"Hey, Krishna, stop trying to look as if butter won't melt in your mouth!"

Oh, how the women scolded him; but it didn't make a jot of difference.

"You enjoy my pranks," Krishna insisted. "Look how they make you laugh!"

Then the women scolded him even more, though behind the cross words, it was quite true, they couldn't conceal their smiles. What a lovable imp he was. But goodness, what a handful for his mother.

Well, in Gokula like everywhere else, the year spun round and the months passed and soon it was nearly time for the rains. Everyone hoped and prayed that the monsoon would come on time and fall not too heavy, not too light. That way the grass would grow thick and green next year, the cows could eat as much as they needed, and the villagers would have plenty of milk to drink.

It was the custom at that season to make offerings to Indra, king of the gods, for it was he who sent rain to the Earth.

When the hour for the ceremony came, the priests lit a special fire and the villagers laid their offerings of fruit, sweets and flowers before it.

The air was fragrant with incense-smoke as the priests chanted their ancient hymns:

> *"Believe in him: he, oh men, is Indra . . .*
> *Even Heaven and Earth bow down before him;*
> *Before his passion even the mountains are afraid . . . "*

Children jostled through the watching crowd, trying to get a better view, climbing on people's shoulders, squeezing through people's legs.

"Sshh! Keep quiet while the priests are chanting!"

But there was one who just would not be still or silent. Who else could it be? Of course, none other than Krishna!

"Hey!" he shouted. "Priests, stop 'your prayers! You've got it all wrong!"

"That boy," murmured the herdsmen, shocked, "needs a good, hard thrashing!"

"Where's his mother?" whispered the milkmaids, horrified. "Why can't she keep him in hand?"

What would the priests say, what would they do? How dared he interrupt their solemn prayers?

But Krishna stood, arms a-kimbo, before the holy men. "I'm not afraid of you!" he declared. "I tell you – stop! Listen to me!"

So the priests stopped and listened. It was a curious thing, but when Krishna asked for something, there was not a soul in all the village who had enough courage to refuse him.

"Look," said Krishna, "why do you pray to Indra? You say he's king of the gods but you've never even seen him! Why do you give him all these wonderful gifts? You say it's his rain that makes the grass grow – but how do you really know?

"If you want to make sacrifices, you ought to make them to the mountain. After all, that's where you can actually see the grass growing. It's the mountain that feeds the cattle that makes the milk for us to drink – not some silly invisible god!"

"He's got a point," somebody muttered, somebody daring. "What's the good of worshipping a god we don't know and can't see?"

"But the sacred books!" exclaimed the priests. "The rituals and hymns of the ancient sages! We must follow tradition as our forefathers did, and their fathers did before them."

"Pooh!" said Krishna. "I'll give you a new tradition. Let's start the tradition of giving gifts to the mountain – our real friend!"

And before anyone could stop him, he had grabbed the biggest dish of sweets and fruits from the sacrifice and was dashing off with it to the slopes.

"Oh! What has that boy done now?"

"Destroying the ancient rituals!"

"Insulting the gods!"

"He'll suffer for it!"

"We'll suffer for it!"

Clutching the sacrificial goods to him, Krishna went running, running, fast as the wind, right up the mountain slopes. Who could catch him? Not his father, not the herdsmen, not the priests, not anyone! It was always impossible to stop Krishna when he was up to one of his pranks.

Everyone just stood there gawping at him. He ran and ran, and did not stop until he was right on the very top.

"Look at me," he shouted, loud enough for everyone to hear him. "I've conquered the mountain! I *am* the mountain!"

He stretched out his arms and legs: up there, glowing in the swirling blue light of the peak, it did indeed look almost as if the mountain were his.

"If I am the mountain," he yelled down at them, "then the mountain is mine, and what's given to the mountain is given to me. Mountain, can I eat the food that the people are offering to you?"

A breeze stirred, shaking the trees, the bushes; even the mountain itself seemed to shake.

"Look!" shouted Krishna, "the mountain is nodding! It says I can eat!"

And with that he broke off a huge piece of the consecrated food that was really meant for Indra and popped it into his mouth.

The crowd watched with a horrified gasp. Whatever punishment would the king of the gods send down upon them now?

Up above the clouds, Indra was sitting on his elephant, polishing thunderbolts. It would soon be time to throw them down to Earth:

no doubt all those wretched humans down there would start moaning and groaning their complaints at him if his rainstorm was late.

Still, there was no harm in keeping them waiting a bit. Better just make sure they were treating him with proper respect before he gave them what they wanted. Let's have a look now . . .

Indra parted the coulds and peered through them to the world below. Yes, there was a village making a handsome sacrifice in his name, and another one there, and another. Good, they were all being suitably humble . . . but hang on, what was going on over there?

The god leaned right over to get a better view. Wasn't that the village of Gokula? Why were the priests standing around looking helpless? What were the people all staring at? And who was that slip of a boy prancing cheekily around on the mountain top, stuffing the most delicious food into his mouth?

"Thundrous Heaven!" Indra spluttered with such anger that he almost fell off his elephant. "That's my food he's eating! The lad's eating the sacrifice the people were offering to me!"

For a few moments the king of the gods just sat there, heaving with indignation until thunder rumbled right across the sky.

"I'll show them!" he roared. "I'll teach them to treat the Rider of the Clouds with such impudence! They want rain do they? Oh, I'll give them rain all right!"

He reached for the biggest, fattest, heaviest bundle of thunder-bolts that he could find, and flung them all together, full force, down to Earth.

Back in Gokula, the villagers heard thunder threatening them across the darkening sky. Lightning crackled. The air grew damp and heavy.

The priests shifted uneasily. Krishna's mother called and coaxed him to come down.

Then it began to rain.

And how it rained. In bucketfuls, in torrents – as if someone were tipping a whole ocean out of the sky.

It splashed onto the parched land, baked so rock-hard by the sun that no water could possibly sink in. Within a few minutes, it began to rise and flood.

Soon it was ankle-deep, knee-deep, thigh-deep. It washed out the sacred fire, swamped the cattle, sent women shrieking to save their belongings from the water-logged houses and huts.

"Krishna, Krishna, now what have you done?" they groaned.

Then suddenly Krishna was back, paddling through the water among them.

"What's the matter?" he laughed. "Why are you all panicking? I've told you, I am the mountain! I'm a match for Indra – I am as mighty as the gods!"

There could hardly be a worse time to mutter such wicked blasphemies! But Krishna could not be silenced.

"Come with me," he urged them, "I'm going to save you."

One by one, the villagers began to realise that he wasn't joking any more. He seemed to have grown, until he was much more than just a boy. His voice was still light, but with promises now, not laughter. It took on a quality that made them stop in their tracks and stare; and when he began to walk away, they all turned to follow.

Krishna waded calmly back to the mountain, while the villagers, wet and bedraggled, trailed through the floods behind.

At the foot of the mountain he crouched down and scrabbled in the earth with his hands.

The mountain began to move! And then . . .

. . . There was a creaking of earth and stone and suddenly, the mountain was floating in the air!

But not quite floating. Something was holding it up. The mountain was balanced on Krishna's finger!

"Come on," he called to the astonished villagers, "bring your cattle and come quickly. There's plenty of room for everyone to shelter here, for as long as there's need to. Now will you believe me when I say that I am mighty? Now will you trust in me to keep you safe?"

So the villagers hurried in and huddled all around him, sheltered from the angry torrents of rain.

They lost track of the hours and days that passed. Balancing the mountain on the tip of his finger, Krishna constantly joked with them and kept them all merry. Yet through all their laughter, they just couldn't help wondering and puzzling: Who was this lad – really? What was he? How did he manage to get away with all the things that he did?

Meanwhile, above the clouds, Indra was jumping up and down with fury. He'd just kept the rain pouring down for seven days and seven nights and he'd almost run out of thunderbolts; but still that rascally Krishna showed no sign of giving up.

Not only that, but it seemed most unlikely he would ever say that he was sorry!

The god leaned back on his elephant, looking thoughtful. Maybe his own power wasn't quite as strong as it used to be.

Maybe . . . it wouldn't do any harm to pop down to Earth and have a quick word with this cheeky, miracle-making lad.

So he slid down through a hole in the Sky to the Earth and went hurrying along to the mountain.

"Hey!" he called. "Come out of there, the lot of you! I've stopped the rain. It's all right – you've won."

All the villagers gasped to see Indra himself, the divine king, appear before them in his glory. Led by the priests they hurried out to do his bidding and flung themselves humbly before his feet.

But Indra, in his impatience, hardly took any notice of them.

"You boy!" he called to Krishna, "put that mountain down! I want to have a word with you."

With a wink at anyone who had eyes to notice, Krishna did as Indra asked him.

"That was a very clever trick," said Indra. "I'm most impressed. You beat me that time, I have to admit. Well then, you owe me something in return, and that's a truthful explanation. Tell me honestly – who are you?"

Krishna grinned. "If I told the villagers they'd never believe me. And yet – the way they all love me despite all I do to them, it's as if they've guessed that I'm more than what I seem."

"Which is?" asked Indra.

"Oh," said Krishna, "you know. The laughter behind the thundercloud. The kiss after the tears. The light that welcomes the traveller out of the darkness." He paused and added softly, "The jewel in the heart of the lotus."

"And if," said Indra equally softly, "if I were to add that you also had more than a little of Lord Vishnu in you, might I perhaps be right?"

"You might," laughed Krishna. "I shan't be the one to say it! But the secret is there, you know, for anyone who wants to find it."

"Hrrmph," said Indra, "then I'm proud to have been defeated by you, my lad. Will you accept if I ask you to be friends?"

But Krishna didn't have time to answer. He was already rushing back to the village, looking out for some new piece of mischief to play.

The Warrior Goddess

The gods were in the most terrible state! All of Heaven had been
over-run by a demon who took the form of a buffalo, and it
seemed there was absolutely nothing that any of them could do
about it.

They had tried, but they simply could not kill him: not with
weapons nor with trickery. Meanwhile, the evil brute was turning the
whole universe up-side-down.

However had the buffalo-demon come by such power?

"It's my fault," admitted Shiva. "Long ago I granted the wretch a
boon."

"Him? A boon!" exclaimed Indra.

"Oh, I didn't realise the evil that was in him at the time," said
Shiva. "In a rash moment, I promised that no one should ever be able
to kill him, except for my own dear wife, Parvati."

"Your wife?" cried Vishnu. "That lovely gentle lady? That divine
mother of the universe? But a woman's business is to protect, not to
go around killing!"

Shiva smiled. "You all know well," he said, "that the moon has a
dark side as well as a bright one. Have you not also seen the dark,
wild side of my own gentle Parvati? If everything were not made of
such opposites, how could the Universe ever be whole?"

The other gods stared at him uncertainly.

"Come with me and see her," Shiva urged them, "and hear what
she has to say."

So they all went to the mountain where Parvati was sitting in a
golden light, combing her long black hair.

51

"Beloved," said Shiva, "we gods have a problem and none but you can overcome it."

Parvati smiled. "Indeed my lord? You had better tell me what it is."

Indra, the king, stepped forward.

"Goddess, there's a buffalo-demon at large in the Universe, and he's stolen paradise out of my very hands! He won't even let me go into my own palace any more. He tramples on all the flower-beds, pollutes the fountains and lounges about the place like a good-for-nothing layabout. And he's stolen my horse – the very king of horses, mark you – and goes about riding it till it foams with exhaustion, like a common nag. To . . . "

Parvati raised her eyebrows at him in mock horror.

"To be quite honest," Indra went on, "I'm surprised to see you sitting here, preening yourself so serenely, lady: did you realise you're the only goddess who still wanders free in all of Heaven? Yes, I thought that would startle you!"

"But what's happened to all the others?" asked Parvati.

"This buffalo-demon has stolen them all, that's what – and works them like servants: he actually makes them do his housework! Can you imagine the humiliation? – and my own dear wife amongst them! Even we gods are at his beck and call. He sends us here and he sends us there: 'do this, do that' he says – and we do it, for we're all so afraid of him, we dare not disobey his commands."

"Weaklings!" cried Parvati. "Not you as well, Lord Shiva? Oh you cowards!"

"The fact is,"said Shiva, "we are caught in a twist of fate. You see, Parvati, it is decreed that none but you can kill this demon."

"I?" exclaimed Parvati. "You want *me* to save you?"

The gods all watched her anxiously. For a few teasing seconds she kept them waiting; then she threw back her head with a golden peal of laughter.

"Oh, have no fear, I shall do what is necessary! Am I not mother of all that's good and bad in the Universe? What, Indra, Brahma, the rest of you, do you think I lack the strength? Fools, what do you know of a woman's power, eh? Do you think I'm all gentle smiles and kisses? Have you never seen the sharpness of a lioness's claws? I tell you, there's a flame of fury that smoulders within me: most times I keep it low, for every woman knows that a caress is better than fighting. But what you tell me, gods, has sparked it off, and I promise that soon you will see it flare beyond your wildest dreams!"

"Your words are encouraging, Parvati," said Indra. "I am happy to leave our fate in your hands."

And with that, the gods went on their way.

Parvati sat thinking for a while, letting the energy gather within her, deciding carefully what to do. Then she whispered a secret spell and turned herself into an enchantress.

If she had been lovely before, now her beauty shone brighter than the stars. Her hair was blue-black like a raven's wing, her skin as rich as cream, her lips and cheeks like wild orchids. Her eyes held all that met them in a trance of wonder; moreover, they could see straight into the depths of anyone's heart.

Then she created a sanctuary on top of the Tawny Mountain, a beautiful paradise-garden where all who entered could live in safety and peace. She surrounded it with a thick hedge of blossom-trees and set four young boys to guard it.

"Do not let anyone enter here or come to me," she told them, "unless they are honest travellers or pilgrims, and you can see for certain that they are suffering from weariness, hunger and thirst."

Meanwhile, the buffalo-demon was wandering through the forests of the Universe, causing terror wherever he went. He seemed to have an insatiable appetite. After every few steps he would suddenly pounce on some innocent animal, kill it with a single bite of his rotting yellow teeth, and gulp it down whole.

Warnings about him soon spread like wild-fire through the forests, and all the animals began to flee as fast and as far as they could. Those who were lucky found themselves by the gates of the wonderful garden of paradise on the Tawny Mountain. There they were welcomed to enter and knew that they would be safe.

But hard on their heels followed the buffalo-demon's evil spies. They too knocked on the garden gates.

"Who goes there?" called the boy-guards; but as soon as they saw the demon-spies, they slammed the gates and shot golden bolts across to bar the way.

However, the demons too had command of magic. They turned themselves into birds and in this form flew over the blossom-hedge into the Tawny Garden. There they roosted secretly in the trees until Parvati came strolling by, disguised in her dazzling enchantment.

They watched breathlessly for as long as they dared, then fluttered away to give news of this wonderment straight to their buffalo master.

"She has eyes like mountain springs and skin as soft as silk, oh master!"

"Her smile would take your breath away!"

"She's as ripe as peaches, slender as a willow . . . "

"Enough, enough!" cried the buffalo-demon, for their descriptions were torturing him with desire. "Just tell me the way to the Tawny Mountain and how I may enter into the garden, then I will see this perfect woman for myself."

So the spies described the lonely path that led to that paradise and how only genuine travellers, harmless, footsore and hungry, were allowed to enter in.

The buffalo turned himself into an old man, carved lines of honest wisdom on his face, and dressed in the humble robes and sandals of a pilgrim. Then he hastened at once to the Tawny Mountain and knocked on the golden gates.

When the boy-guards saw such an ancient, dusty pilgrim standing on the threshold, they flung the gates wide open and even called the goddess herself to honour him with a greeting.

Parvati came strolling gracefully through the scented, dewy shrubs. In the instant that she saw the old pilgrim she knew him for what he really was; but narrowing her sparkling eyes, she said nothing.

"Greetings, lady," said the old man, bowing very low. "What a wonderful garden you have here! But tell me, why do you stay in this lonely place when the whole world would be charmed to have a sight of your beauty?"

"Ah," said the goddess, "I have vowed to stay here until I find a man who is good enough for me to marry."

"Madam," cried the old pilgrim, "you have found him now! Yes, yes, I know I am bent and lined with the years – but you do not know yet who I am! I am the most powerful man in the Universe! I hold the Three Worlds in the palm of my hand!

"Tell me what is your heart's desire, lady, for I can give you anything you want. I have nine treasure-houses overflowing with wonderful things. I have a thousand servants waiting to be at your beck and call. There is nothing you might imagine or dream of, that I cannot give you."

He leered towards Parvati.

"Come, come, only tell me what you wish for, my beauty. Choose something you believe to be impossible. Let me grant it for you, to prove beyond doubt how powerful I am; and then in return promise you will be my wife."

The goddess opened her eyes wide.

"Good sir," said she, "if you are really so supreme, what better man could I hope to find for a husband? Now let me see, whatever can I possibly wish for? Ah yes, I know. I wish you to turn yourself into a woman."

"A woman?" cried the pilgrim. "You want me to become a woman? Pah! whatever do you take me for?"

"A magician, surely," said Parvati calmly. "You have just told me that everything lies within your power."

"Why, I'd sooner turn myself into a worm than a measly, worthless female!" snarled the old man. "What a pathetic wish! Oh yes, you're right, I am a magician indeed, and a master of changes. This is my true form!"

All at once, he was not an old man any more, but the buffalo-demon, huge and monstrous, rising up to strike the goddess down!

"Worthless?" shrieked Parvati. "Pathetic? I'll show you who's worthless! This is *my* true form, Demon: know that I am also Durga, she whom no one can overcome!"

And with that, she turned herself into a blinding sheet of fire.

"Oh, but you are still not as great as me, Parvati or Durga, whatever they call you!" roared the demon; and at once he was a mountain, broad and towering, unyielding as rock.

"Where are you, all you blundering gods in Heaven?" called the goddess. "Come and share your strength with me, hurry, hurry, if you wish me to get rid of this evil one!"

From all directions, the gods came running to her. Now she was a woman again, but her beauty was sharp as diamonds, her power shot out like lightning, channelled into ten angry arms.

"Give me all your weapons!"

Shiva and Vishnu, Brahma, Indra, Agni and all the other gods hastened to obey. Now her ten hands clutched thunderbolts and daggers, tridents, lances, spears and swords; and the flames of her fury lit the sky.

"Come now, Buffalo!" she shrieked. "Fight me if you dare!"

The demon charged and struck her with his muzzle, trampled her with his hooves, lashed her with his tail. All around the gods watched, petrified; but the goddess was not afraid.

He pierced her with his horns, rushed round her like a whirlwind; he blew his breath at her like a hurricane that hurled her to the ground.

But the goddess only laughed at him.

The demon pounded the Earth till it screamed under his hooves, he tossed the mountains on his horns till they shattered the clouds into fragments; he stirred the ocean with his tail into a frothing frenzy of floods on every side.

The goddess watched, rejoicing, for the more evil he made the more she hated him, and the more certain she grew that she would win.

The demon turned himself into a lion; with one blow, the goddess sliced off his head.

The demon turned himself into an elephant; the goddess slashed off his trunk with a sword.

The demon turned back into his own form, the buffalo: drunk with strength, he shook the Three Worlds, wrenched up mountains by their roots and hurled them at the goddess.

But she was drunk too, on blood, wine and anger. She mashed the mountain missiles to pulp with a hail of her own fiery arrows. Then she ran at the demon and leaped onto his back: he reared up with a bellow that reached beyond the edge of the Universe. Kicking him, beating him, the goddess gave a shriek of triumph, then thrust the prongs of her trident straight into his heart.

His last scream pierced beyond every shade of terror; then his evil blanked out, as a cloud obliterates the moon.

Parvati threw down her weapons, still angry, yet ever soft and tender; and with a single smile at the gods, strode regally away to bathe and comb her hair.

Doom of the
Magic Cities

There were once three demon brothers called Taraksa, Kamalaksa and Vidyunmalin who decided to give up the wickedness of their forefathers and devote their lives to doing good. For many years they went without any worldly pleasures, and gave whatever luxuries came their way either to the poor or as offerings to the gods.

From his seat in Heaven, Brahma saw them and was delighted. What a pleasant surprise for a bunch of demons to behave themselves so well! They certainly deserved a reward.

So he went down to Earth to pay them a visit.

Taraksa, Kamalaksa and Vidyunmalin were beside themselves with excitement when the mysterious Lord of Creation suddenly appeared before them. They bowed down low at his feet, but the god dismissed them with a wave of his four hands.

"No no," he said, "today I have come to honour you! Brothers, you have pleased me well by living such good lives, and because of this I shall grant you a boon. So tell me what thing you wish for."

At first the three demons were so astonished that they could not think what to say. They whispered amongst themselves for a while; and then Taraksa said, "Holy Grandfather, this is what we would like: the gift of eternal life; the promise that we three shall live forever."

But Brahma shook his four heads.

"No," he said, "you wish for something beyond the power even of the gods. No living being in all the Three Worlds can ever be truly immortal. You must choose something different."

So the brothers whispered secretly again; and this time Kamalaksa was their spokesman.

"Grandfather, perhaps you may see fit to fulfil a worldly dream that for many years has haunted us. We would each like to found a magnificent city on Earth, and we would like these cities to grow in power and splendour with we three as rulers for the span of a thousand years. Lord, we know that after that period we and our cities must come to an end, for that is the way of all things; but when the time comes, grant us this last favour: may we be honoured by a quick destruction, with a single arrow from the mightiest of all the gods."

"That is a good wish," said Brahma, "and an interesting one. I shall see that you achieve what you long for. But remember this: use it well and do not get so drunk with power that you forget your good intentions."

And with that he climbed back on his feathered goose and winged his way back to Heaven.

The three brothers could hardly believe their luck. What a boon to be granted! At once they rushed off to discuss their plans, and soon they had arranged for the best architect in the world to design their cities and to take charge of the building.

It was a long, slow task; but at last the three cities were all complete, and what marvels they were indeed.

Taraksa's city was built entirely of sparkling gold, and its streets were bright as the sun.

Kamalaksa's city was built all of shimmering silver, and its houses were filled with soft light, such as that which shines from the moon.

Vidyunmalin's city was built of fine black iron, and all its buildings and by-ways were strong and safe as the mountains.

As Brahma had promised, the three cities grew quickly in size, power and splendour. As their reputation spread, more and more people wanted to go and live in them, and soon each was one hundred leagues long and one hundred leagues wide. They were brimming over with beautiful houses and brilliant palaces, well kept gardens, ornamental gates, amusement halls and plenty of spacious parks. The air above them grew rich with music, laughter and the jingling of money, so that the city dwellers began to joke that their very streets were touched with magic.

Indeed, before long, it seemed that everyone in the world wanted to live in one of those cities. It became the fashion for families to pack their belongings, leave their humble huts in the country and move into one of the shining new houses in town. Who wanted to live like a moth-eaten peasant when the demons had brought the good life within everyone's easy reach?

In this way, soon the whole Earth was ruled by the three demon brothers and their powers of iron, silver and gold.

Now, perhaps it was only rumours or perhaps it was really true, but it began to be said that many of those who went to live in the three cities were turning into demons themselves. Of course, it is not always easy to recognise a demon just by the look of him. But this is why the rumours arose: one after another, the wonderful streets were overtaken by wickedness, ugliness and crime.

Houses were broken into by burglars; people were attacked and robbed as they did their shopping or walked in the park. Sinister looking men took to lurking at alleys and corners, terrorising the women. Vandals broke pieces off the beautiful carvings which graced the city temples, and daubed rude words across paintings of the gods. Even the countryside beyond the city walls was not safe, for at holidays and festivals, parties went out chopping down trees for picnic fires, uprooting wildflowers and bringing terror to the lives of animals by hunting them in a bloodbath of sport.

In the City of Gold a group of people got together who felt that things were getting out of hand, and went to see Taraksa, their demon king.

"Your majesty," they said, "we know well that your power was granted by the gods, so how can you allow it to be abused in this way? Great king, don't you realise that this whole city is over-run by decadence and violence?"

"Nonsense, nonsense!" cried King Taraksa. "Go away and enjoy yourselves! Everything in the cities and the world around them exists entirely for everyone's pleasure!"

But after they had gone, Taraksa thought quietly to himself, *It is not a good thing when my people start to criticise. I must show them that the gods are still on our side.*

So he called his son Hari to him, saying, "Go and devote yourself to the gods for a while, my lad, just as I and your two uncles did when we were young. Live a good, old fashioned, upright life until you have won yourself a boon. And when the boon is offered to you, Hari, be sure to choose it carefully. Ask for a gift that the whole world may see and admire, so that it is plain to all that we still have Heaven's approval."

Hari was a bright lad, and he saw the sense in doing as his father told him. So for many years he went without worldly pleasures and gave whatever luxuries came his way either to the poor, or as offerings to the goods.

Once again, Brahma looked down from Heaven and was well pleased. He visited Hari on Earth and offered him a boon as a reward.

"Grandfather," said the young man, "I have thought carefully and this is what I wish for. In my father's Golden City there is a lake. I ask you to give the waters of that lake such power that if people who have been wounded in battle should bathe in it, they will come out with twice the health and twice the strength that they had before."

"You have chosen well," said Brahma. "It is a good thing to ask

60

that the injured should be healed. What you request shall be granted."

And with that, the Lord Creator flew on his goose back to Heaven.

The Magic Lake in the Golden City was soon tried, tested and proven. Word got around about its wonderful powers and how anyone in the Cities of Silver and Iron, as well as in the City of Gold, was openly welcome to use it.

"Yes, come and wash away your wounds!" cried King Taraksa and Prince Hari to battle-scarred warriors, to street fighters and wrestlers. "Everything here in our three cities, as you well know, exists entirely for everyone's pleasure."

The Magic Lake grew so famous and popular that people no longer had any fear of being hurt. It was marvellous to know that, no matter how badly someone was injured, they would would make a miraculous recovery in its healing waters.

As a result, people were no longer afraid to turn arguments into full-scale battles. Neighbours who fell out over the silliest things took to bashing each other's heads in; and then queued up side by side to bathe themselves better in the Magic Lake. Gangs of children made brutal attacks on each other for a handful of marbles or a bagful of sweets while their parents looked on smiling, for a swim to wash away the bruises in the magic waters was a popular family outing. People whipped their sons till they bled, then sent them to the Lake to become twice as strong as they were beforehand. They even smacked and pushed their grandmothers about, then sent them off for a holiday by the magic waters, promising this would make the old ladies live forever!

Things got worse and worse. The three cities declared war on each other just for fun, and invented the most dreadful weapons, knowing that their injured armies could go to the Lake and emerge ready to fight, over and over again.

Up in Heaven the gods saw what was going on and began to fret.

"These demons are ruining the whole Earth," declared Indra. "They have lost all sense of what is right and good. They must be destroyed!"

He called the seven storm gods to his side, the ones who ride on the wind, and together they began to hurl torrents of thunderbolts down onto the Earth. But the Gold, Silver and Iron Cities stood proud and strong, repelling even Indra's terrible weapons.

In a fury, the king of the gods went to see Brahma.

"Grandfather," he shouted, "what foolish magic have you created down there on Earth? Even with all my thunderbolts I can't make a dent in this mountain of wickedness. Tell me how I can destroy it."

Brahma thought back a thousand years to when he had granted the three demon brothers their boon. Certainly he had not promised that they would be indestructible. What was the condition he had agreed?

"Ah, that was it," he remembered, "when the time comes for their end, they and their cities must be destroyed quickly with a single arrow shot by the mightiest of all the gods."

Indra listened in silence. "So," he said, "shall I succeed with one arrow where all my thunderbolts have failed?"

"That arrow will not come from you, Indra," said Brahma quickly. "Great as you are, oh King of Rain and Thunder, know that you are not the mightiest in all the Heavens. No, the time has come to seek the help of one so great that his very breath can send the stars and planets dancing; the one whose third eye burns with the heat of the sun; the one whom all living beings love yet tremble to speak of. So spread this word throughout Heaven, Indra: we must go and ask Lord Shiva to save us – the great Destroyer!"

Even the gods were rather nervous of Shiva, but when Indra told them what the Grandfather had said, they knew that he was right. So together they went looking here and there until they found him, sitting on a mountain, lost in deepest thought.

Snakes were twined around the sinews of his lithe, ash-pale body. Moonlight danced like water through strands of his long, wild hair. But he looked up and smiled warmly when the gods called out their greeting.

"You have come to ask something of me, my friends," he said. "What is it you want?" He smiled again. "Come now, tell me, tell me."

So Brahma explained about the demons, the Three Cities and the Magic Lake; and the boons by which he had brought them into being.

"I have given these Earth dwellers too much," he said. "The truth is, Lord Shiva, none but you has power enough to destroy them."

"Wait," said Shiva, "I do not wish to make my dance of destruction right now. I am too busy thinking. Perhaps this will be enough to help you: I will give you half of my own energy to add to your weapons. Take this power of mine and use it yourselves to bring the Three Cities to their doom."

"Lord and master," cried Indra, "even this is not enough! I plead with you as King of Heaven and tell you this – I have tried and wasted a thousand of my own explosive thunderbolts already and they have bounced off the demons' glittering cities as if they had no more strength in them than flies. We beg you to do as the holy Grandfather asks you – for so it is written in the book of fate – the time has come to destroy the demons and the fortresses they have built, and none but Lord Shiva can do it."

Shiva stood up with a sigh, unwinding his strong limbs until they blazed, blinding white, across the Heavens. He tossed back his head and with his fingers combed the moonlit water from his tangled hair. He stooped a little, weighed down by the burden of his own might.

"Very well," he said, "then I must do it." The smile still played around his mouth, but now it was touched with the grimness of danger. "But friends, I ask you this – give me some of your own energy to add to my power, for I cannot risk failure in this mission."

"You may take what you want of us, lord and master," said the gods with one voice.

So Lord Shiva made an arrow with Agni the fire god as its shaft and Vishnu the Lord Protector as its head. He mounted a chariot made from the body of the goddess Earth, and hung it about with rainbows and lightning. Then he rode forth through a furnace of energy that was hotter than ten thousand exploding suns: rode straight towards the Earth and the Cities of Iron, Silver and Gold.

As he rode, the Earth began to burn and tremble, so that the three demon kings grew afraid. They ended their war-games and ordered their subjects to stop all other fighting in the city streets. Sensing some terrible danger that threatened them all, they signed peace treaties and made the Three Cities into One.

One world it was now; but a world where evil magic dripped from every corner, whose darkness was deeper than the light of all the gods.

Shiva rode on and on towards it, and what he saw stirred him to a frenzy of savage anger.

With a roar that shook the cosmos, he drew back his bow and shot an arrow straight to the heart of the Earth.

In a flash, black flames seared through the Triple City!

It was gone, gone, gone! Where for a thousand years the demon brothers had ruled over silver, gold and iron, now there was nothing, no one: only a desert of pale, steaming ashes.

Softly, a wind blew. The sun set, red and peaceful, beyond the edge of the Western Ocean.

But faintly, under the ashes, an earthly heart was still beating. The waters settled and the sands of Time shifted. The gods went home to Heaven, contented. Clean and new, the next Age would soon begin.

The Filthy Giant

Narkasur had a mother who loved him, but despite that, he was a horrible specimen, even as demons go.

For a start, he was a giant, twice as tall, twice as broad and twice as fat as ordinary mortal men. Not that he could help that, of course (apart from the fatness); but the worst of it was that he was dirty. Not just ordinary dirty, but disgustingly filthy. He hadn't had a wash since the day that he was born. He had never, ever, not once in all his life, cleaned his house, so that it was knee-high in dust and cockroaches, piled up with rubbish, full of unmentionable things. And it stank. It was enough to make anyone feel quite ill if they dared to go anywhere near it.

Now, it would have been Narkasur's own private business that he chose to live in such squalor, if only he had kept himself to himself. But he did not. He could not stand living all alone. He loved company – particularly the company of beautiful girls and women.

Not surprisingly, there was not a lady alive who would willingly have been his companion, so Narkasur had to get women into his house by rather devious means. To be quite frank, he kidnapped them. He loved dragging them home, one by one, with their long black hair and wild, frightened eyes and the dusky softness of their skin.

Narkasur soon decided that stealing women was his very greatest pleasure: in fact, it was an obsession. He thought of them as his 'little collection'. One day, he decided to count how many he had – and found that there were exactly sixteen thousand girls and women in all.

What did he do with them? Well, sometimes he pulled them out to admire and tease, but most of the time he just made them stay in the foul-smelling, damp, filthy darkness of his dungeaon.

How they wept and screamed down there! And how evil Narkasur loved to hear them! He used to stand gazing down at them from the dungeon steps, listening to their shrill cries that were like the heart-wrenching music of caged birds.

"Keep on twittering, it makes me laugh, my little sad-eyed beauties!" he roared. And then he went away and slammed the trap-door shut.

"Oh, oh, oh!" they wailed, stepping gingerly over the rotting rubbish, holding their noses against the sickening stench. "Whatever shall we do? Whatever will become of us? What sins have we committed to be condemned to this dreadful hell?"

Now, amongst the sixteen thousand there was one woman who was more beautiful than all the rest. Her skin was golden, and even in that stinking place, she radiated the sweet perfume of lotus-blossom. She was graceful and slender, and though her eyes were bright, it was not with tears.

"Stop your weeping and moaning, sisters," she urged the others. "How do you suppose that can possibly help you? There's only one hope we have of saving ourselves – and that's to call upon the gods. Think of Lord Vishnu! Doesn't he love and protest all the innocent? Then let's give him our trust and pray to him together."

She spoke so surely and so serenely that at this thought the others were persuaded to dry their eyes. Whispers went around: this was no mortal woman, but a goddess whom Narkasur had somehow stolen. Surely it was not possible: could it really be Lakshmi, Vishnu's own wife, guardian and bringer of good fortune? If it were her indeed, if she were missing from Heaven, no wonder such darkness had entered their lives!

So they turned their hearts to Heaven calling as if with one voice from all their thousands:

"Lord Vishnu, Vishnu, please help us! Hear us, have mercy and save us, dearest Lord!"

Now it so happened that Lord Vishnu heard their prayer at once; for he was not up in Heaven after all, but already wandering the Earth. In that Age, he had been born, you might remember, as Krishna, son of a cowherd. All through his youth, he had been full of mischief; but now he was grown, his purpose was clear: to restore the power of good.

Across thousands of miles he heard the women crying. He looked, and in his mind's eye, he saw the filthy giant and the squalor in which the women lay trapped.

At once, he set off to save them, travelling across the whole breadth of India until he reached the gates of Narkasur's lair.

"Ho!" cried a terrible voice when he got there. "Stop! Only women may enter!"

Krishna stopped and very soon the owner of the voice appeared. It looked even more awful that it had sounded: a great, lumbering monster with five hideous heads.

"Ho!" cried the monster again, "I am Mura. I have instructions to kill invaders such as you." It belched and bellowed like a boar. "What do you say to that, you miserable sliver of a man?"

"I say I am more than a man and I shall kill you first!" replied Krishna; and with that they flung themselves into a fight.

They fought with fists and they fought with weapons, so fiercely that even in the depths of Narkasur's dungeon the women felt the ground shake and heard the fury of their groans.

At last, Krishna drove his lance into the monster's heart and watched it fall dead at his feet.

Now he wandered through the alleys and passages of the stinking lair, treading everywhere on piles of filth. Rats clawed amongst the rubbish, flies buzzed around puddles of stagnant liquid. Then suddenly, looming up from the depths of his squalor, came the filthy demon himself.

"Ha!" cried he, towering above the god. "What are you doing here, you miserable monster killer? This is my place! Keep out! Would you dare to interfere with mighty Narkasur and intrude on my little games? What shall I do with you, worm?"

"You shall fight me, giant!" cried Krishna, "for no man on Earth may own any place that does not also belong to me."

And with that he flung himself into battle again.

If it had been hard to defeat the five-headed monster, it was harder still to overcome Narkasur, with his rippling leathery muscles set in his huge, towering frame.

They fought with fists and they fought with weapons; the ground trembled for a hundred leagues around. Then at last the god stepped back and hurled his discus, full force, straight into Narkasur's face.

The giant gave a yell of pain; he staggered back, swayed a moment, then crumpled to the dirt-smeared ground. He began to bleat and groan piteously, pathetically, like a great, fat overgrown baby.

"Mother!" he whimpered, "oh Mu . . . Mu . . . Mother, come quickly! I'm dying! I hurt! Ow . . . "

At this, a fat old woman came shuffling along .

"What's going on, what's up?" she muttered; then she caught sight of Narkasur. "Oh my son!" she cried, "oh my poor little boy! What has this nasty villain done to you?"

"Mother," moaned Narkasur, "he's broken his way in and slain my monster and now I think he's killed me too! Oh! Ow! Oh!"

"You wretch!" exclaimed the woman, turning to Krishna. "You vicious, interfering bully! Listen, this murder you've committed won't go forgotten, oh no! I shall make a curse for the world to remember it by for ever, and this is it: *May the sorrow you've brought through the death of my son be avenged by . . .* "

"Wait!" Krishna interrupted her, "you do not know yet who I am!"

Then he flung back his cloak to reveal the true face of his divinity, in all its splendour and glory.

The old woman gave a cry and hid her face from his dazzling blue light; she took a step backwards and stuffed a trembling hand into her mouth.

"It's the gods!" she exclaimed. "The gods have come to walk amongst us! Narkasur, my boy, what have you done to bring such a thing on your poor, humble old mother?"

"Oh, a sin," whimpered Narkasur, clutching his wounds and writhing in agony under Krishna's brilliant gaze. "Mother, I've got sixteen thousand sins stored away in the depths of my dungeon! By my soul, mother, please help me to make up for them all before I die!"

The old woman shook her head. Tears welled up in her sunken, yellow eyes. Silently she knelt by her gigantic Narkasur, stroking his blood-stained hair.

"I shall have to try and make up for them in the only way I can think of," she said, "for I can see there is not much time. I shall turn the curse I intended into a blessing. So hear this, oh mighty god: *May the sorrow you've brought through the death of my son be avenged by spreading happiness to every corner of the Earth.*"

Krishna nodded. "That is a good memorial," he said. "So, Narkasur: what do you have to say to that?"

"Oh yes, yes, let it be so, lord!" cried the giant. "Let everyone celebrate my death and the sin it removes from the world!"

"That," said Krishna, "is even better." Then he knelt down and withdrew the last breath from Narkasur like a sword gently from its sheath, so that the demon came to his end in peace.

"Come," said Krishna soothingly to the weeping old mother, "let me finish the deed I have come to do and wipe away the last of his evil. Tell me the way to your son's dark dungeon."

"It is through there," said Narkasur's mother, pointing through the dusty maze of dirt-ridden passages. "There is a key hanging on a hook by the door; but what you will find inside I don't know and certainly don't want to imagine . . ."

When the sixteen thousand kidnapped women heard the key turn in the lock and the great dungeon door heave creaking open, they all began to tremble; for each was terrified that it would be her own turn to suffer the giant's cruel torments. But instead . . .

"Oh!"

"What is this?"

"Sisters, a miracle, a vision!"

"It's true – our prayers have been answered!"

One by one they turned to look and saw, not the demon-giant standing there, but their beloved blue-skinned god!

"Follow me," he called to them, "and quickly. No no, I beg you, this is no time to stop and worship me! I have come to bring you freedom. Dance all the way home to your husbands and fathers! For Narkasur is dead – and he wishes that this should make all creation happy!"

From under his cloak, Krishna took out his flute and began to play.

"This is the path to liberty, sweet ladies! Walk the way that I lead you and make your hearts smile and dance again!"

Then to the haunting notes of his celestial music he led them, with golden Lakshmi at their head, up the steps and out of the dungeon, through the fortress and out through the gates, back to a world whose joy shone out at their coming like a million twinkling lights!

The Slaying of
the Dragon

Once a humble woodcutter was busy at his work when he heard an almighty disturbance on the other side of the forest. So he slung his axe over his shoulder and strode whistling through the trees to take a look at what was going on.

By and by, he came to a clearing, and what he saw there drew him up with a start. For an enormous man was lying dead on the ground – a giant with three heads. Standing over him, with a dangerous gleam in his eye, was a second man, carrying a strange bag of weapons and bathed in a curious halo of light.

The woodcutter, being a down-to-earth type of fellow, had always vowed to keep clear of anything that he did not understand. So he was about to hurry away before his presence was noticed, when suddenly a thundrous voice called after him:

"Wait! Come back! I command you to give me your help!"

The woodcutter turned slowly round, dazzled by the stranger's light.

"What is it that you want of me?" he mumbled, staring nervously at the ground.

"You seem like a fine, strong fellow," said the other, "and that axe of yours looks nice and sharp. What I want, is for you to step forward with it and chop off this giant's three heads."

"But . . . but . . . " protested the woodcutter, stammering in his alarm, "I can't!"

"Whyever not?" demanded the stranger.

"Be . . . because the giant's necks are thicker than any tree that I've ever seen," said the woodcutter, seizing the first excuse that

entered his mind, "and I'm sure my axe will never go through them."

"Oh, if that's the only problem," said the stranger, "we can easily overcome it. Give me your word that you'll do as I say, and I'll make your axe as sharp as the ice that tops the Himalayas!"

The woodcutter grew more suspicious than ever. What kind of magic was this that he had stumbled upon? He stared at the stranger's shadow.

"Who are you?" he whispered. And then: "Was it you who killed the giant?"

The stranger drew himself up tall and let the light fall away so that now the woodcutter could clearly see his face.

"I am Indra, king of the gods."

The woodcutter's mouth dropped open. He tried to speak, but no words came.

"And yes, it was I who killed him."

"But . . . but . . . that's murder!" stammered the woodcutter foolishly. He sneaked a glance at the terrible, three-headed body. "And look, he's wearing the saffron robes of a priest! You, Lord of all Heaven, committing the highest crime of priest-murder? Surely the gods are above such sin! I thought . . . " He fell to his knees, weak with confusion. "Why, Lord Indra . . . ? Oh, forgive me, I'm only a poor, ignorant man: how can I hope to understand the ways of the gods?"

"Listen," said Indra. "This giant – this priest as you call him – had grown so strong and powerful that I feared he would throw me off my very own throne and take over the Triple Universe! Yes, friend, even I, the king of Heaven, am afraid of such a mighty demon."

"A demon?" exclaimed the woodcutter. "Is it really possible to be a demon as well as a priest?"

"Such deceits are all too common," said Indra gravely. "But, lucky mortal that you are, I can see you have no experience of the battle between evil and good."

The cutter shook his head.

"Well, take this wisdom in return for what you must do for me," said Indra. "Things and even people are not always as they seem. Remember that and think on it. Now let me tell you more about the fate that befell this demon. For you see, before I decided to kill him, I tried to weaken his power and purpose by gentle means. I tried my utmost to make him fall in love."

The woodman listened, goggle-eyed.

"I sent a hundred of Heaven's prettiest nymphs to dance before him," Indra went on, "and to shower him with their kisses. But they could not move him: his heart and his purpose stayed firm as rock. That is when I realised just how mighty and dangerous he was, and decided he would have to die."

He nudged the enormous, ugly body gingerly with his foot.

"His death was quick and painless, for I stabbed him with a thunderbolt. But, Woodcutter, though his heart has stopped and his brain is still, I still feel scorched by the evil energy that pours out of him. It worries me. Come here and feel for yourself the heat that still burns in his three heads."

The woodcutter did as Indra told him, and felt the force of the giant's heat. He folded his palms and bowed humbly before the great god.

"Lord," he said, "your will must be my duty. I shall try to cut off these terrible heads, just as you have asked me."

Then he lifted his axe, feeling it grow heavy and sharp as ice in his hand. He swung it down, hard as he could, on the first of the giant's necks.

Saaap! The head fell clean from the body – and from the wound a great flock of heathcocks flew out.

Then he swung his axe down on the second of the giant's necks.

Saaap! The head fell clean from the body – and from the wound a cloud of partridges fluttered away.

Then he swung his axe on the third of the giant's necks.

Saaap! The head fell clean from the body – and from the wound a chattering of sparrows darted off in all directions.

"You have done well, Cutter," said Indra happily, "and I promise you this: the Three Worlds shall know that this deed of yours was no sin but an act of purest devotion and goodness to fulfil the will of Heaven. Now one one thing I ask you: do not tell anyone what has passed between us."

"What the king of the gods commands, I cannot help but obey," murmured the woodcutter.

Indra smiled and dismissed him with a wave of his hand; and with a troubled heart, the cutter hurried back to his work.

A year passed. The woodcutter, true to his promise, spoke to no one. But somehow rumour began to fly like ghosts about the Universe: *Indra is a priest-murderer. The king of gods has committed a terrible sin!*

Indra was ashamed. He took a vow of penance and slipped down from Heaven to wander about the Earth. For a long time he lived in disguise as a mortal beggar, until he had purged himself of the terrible crime he had done. At last, the sin spilled out of him: he divided it up and hid some in the sea, some in the soil and some in the trees. Then, feeling clean and pure once more, he returned to his throne in Heaven.

But every deed sets a wheel of fate in motion, and so it was when Indra had killed the giant with three heads. For there was one who could never forget or forgive him, and that was the giant's father.

Stricken with grief, consumed by fury, the father created a demon in the shape of a dragon. He made its thoughts dark as underground pools, with vengeance straight from the heart of its master: *Indra must be killed, I must destroy the king of the gods!*

So the dragon hurried to Heaven like the fiery sun of Doomsday, hot on the scent of Indra. In every realm it passed through, its poisoned breath defiled water, light and air.

It reached Indra's throne with a bloodcurdling roar. At once the king of the gods reached urgently for his thunderbolts; but before he could get hold of them, the dragon opened its mouth and in one burning gulp swallowed him right up!

The other gods saw what had happened and were filled with terror. In desperation they wove all their magic powers together and made the dragon yawn.

Creeping up through the red chambers of its belly, Indra felt it stretch and saw a sudden gape of daylight, at the far end of the tunnel-like throat. He gathered himself up and with all his strength leaped out cleanly through its cavernous mouth.

He was safe, but with no time to waste. He dashed to seize a fistful of thunderbolts, then turned back bravely to face the dragon.

And so they fought; but before long Indra realised to his horror and shame that he was losing. In despair he persuaded the demon to agree to a pause in the fighting; then he retreated to the other gods and asked for advice as to what he should do.

"Above all else," said Vishnu, "we must protect your life, King. So if you cannot overcome this dragon, the only solution is to make a treaty of peace between you. I will find a party of wise mortal men to act as diplomats in the Earthly manner, and get them to persuade your enemy to agree."

So the Lord Preserver went to Earth where he looked from end to end for the greatest sages he could find.

"Come with me," he told them, "I have a sacred task for you."

Then he whisked them to Heaven without further ado. There he sent them straight to the dragon and told them to give it this message:

"Oh mighty one, we come to beg you to make your peace. No one can overcome you, in all of Earth or Heaven. The whole Universe is in your power except for the King of Heaven himself, and you must know that he can never be conquered. This is what we humbly urge you: make a pact of friendship with Indra, and end this useless violence between you for once and for all."

The dragon looked at the sages and saw that wisdom lay in their words just as it was carved on their ancient faces.

"Mortals," said he, "what you say makes good sense. In conquering the Universe I have more than avenged the giant's death for his father, and I have wearied myself with fighting. Yes, I shall make peace with Indra – if he will agree to one condition."

"And what is that?" enquired the sages.

"The condition is this: that I shall never be killed by any known weapon, by anything dry or anything wet, by day or or by night, on water or on land. If King Indra will guarantee my life in this way, then I will agree to make my peace."

And so it was that the pact was made. The dragon returned to its maker, Indra to his throne and the sages went back to Earth.

Time passed. There was peace and stillness in the Universe. Yet above the clouds, fingering his thunderbolts, Indra remained uneasy. So long as the dragon roamed free, his throne could not be safe.

He took to wandering here and there, in the wake of where the dragon wandered, spying on it, looking for a loophole in their pact of peace.

At last the moment came.

He saw the demon walking on the seashore – neither on water nor on land!

And it was sunset – that strange twilight hour which is neither day nor night!

Quickly, feverishly, Indra searched for something he might use to destroy it, a thing that was neither wet nor dry, nor recognisable as any weapon – and at that moment, on the crest of a wave, he saw a great mass of mountainous foam!

Swifter than his own lightning, Indra rushed out and seized the foam. He stood on the sea–strand in the twilight and hurled it full force at the dragon.

It found its mark, the pact was broken and at last the long chain of evil was destroyed.

The Princess and the Ten-Headed Demon

Whenever King Janaka looked at his daughter Sita, he used to shake his head in happy wonder.

"That I should have produced a child of such grace and beauty!" he used to murmur. "And one so kind and gentle: I declare I've never once heard a cross word from her lips, nor seen an angry thought furrow her brow. What a blessing she is to me!"

And sometimes, when he was sure of being quite alone, he would whisper to the corners and shadows of his palace: "It is almost as if the goddess Lakshmi had come to live amongst us! But no, it is impossible that such a thing should be."

Well, the years passed until it was time for Princess Sita to marry. But however would Janaka find a husband who was good enough for her? He worried and thought about it for many days; and at last decided that he would have to set a near–impossible test.

So he had a gigantic bow made, with a string that was even tougher and less supple than iron. Then he let it be known throughout his kingdom that if any man were mighty enough to bend that bowstring, Princess Sita would be his wife.

Many suitors came from near and far, but not one could find success, until one day two princes were shown into the palace.

"Greetings, your majesty," said the younger. "My name is Lakshmana, and this is my noble brother Rama. We are the sons of your neighbour, King Dasharatha. I have just persuaded Prince Rama to take up your famous challenge.

King Janaka looked at Rama. He was well-built and upright, quiet in his bearing, and a noble light shone from his eyes. He thought to himself, *Now here is one surely touched with the grace of the gods*; but to those around him he said nothing.

Instead, he led the princes out to the courtyard and called to his servants to make things ready.

There came the sound of heavy wheels rumbling, growing closer. Then two enormous carved gates swung open; and in marched one-hundred-and-fifty strong men, hauling an enormous eight-wheeled chariot that sagged under the weight of the mighty bow.

"Prince Rama," said the king wearily, for he had been through this scene many times before, "there it is. Bend the bowstring and Princess Sita shall be yours."

Rama stepped up to it. He closed his lean fingers around it and drew them back.

A gasp flew round the courtyard: he had bent the string, he had done it.

Then the gasps were lost in a loud CRACK as the bow snapped clean in half.

"Quickly!" exclaimed Janaka, beside himself with excitement. "Somebody fetch my daughter!"

But at that very moment, Sita herself came running out to see whatever was going on.

In one glance she took in the scene: the broken bow and handsome Rama standing modestly beside it. Then their eyes met; and for an instant the whole courtyard spun thundrously with the shock of love.

"I think," said King Janaka in a shaky voice, "that he must be the one we have been waiting for all this time." He cleared his throat carefully. "Dear Sita, Prince Rama . . . I am so glad! May I begin to fix your wedding at once?"

So Rama and Sita were married. Everyone said how devoted and charming they were; and was it not fortunate that Rama's old, sick father, King Dasharatha, had such excellent heirs to his throne?

But one day, Sita found Rama sitting silently shaking, hiding his face in his hands.

"My love," she cried, "Whatever is the matter?"

Rama looked up.

"Sweet princess, my father is on his death bed."

"Oh Rama, if only I could comfort you! Be brave, dear husband: you know that all who live must die, and one day his good soul will be born again."

The prince sighed long and deeply. "Oh, but it is not just this that weighs me down. I have something much worse to tell you. Sita, as soon as my father dies I have to leave you, for I shall be banished at once into exile."

"But that's impossible! You will be the new king!"

"Not any longer. Everything has changed. There have been plots . . ."

"Tell me what's going on!"

Rama looked sadly at his gentle wife.

"You know my step-mother, Queen Kaikeyi? She is a scheming, jealous woman. Last week she went to my father while he was lying in bed, sweating with fever and said, 'Dasharatha, long ago I saved your life and in return you promised to grant me two wishes.'

" 'Oh yes,' said my father, 'I remember it well.'

" 'As yet,' said my stepmother, 'I have never wished for anything; but now I see I had better claim what you promised before it is too late.'

" 'Well,' said my father, 'it is my holy duty to keep any promise I made to my wife. Tell me what you want.'

" 'This,' said my stepmother. 'Firstly, that high and mighty Rama should be banished to the forest for fourteen years; and secondly, that in his place my own son, Prince Bharata, shall be king.' "

"Oh the scheming witch!" cried Sita. "I can hardly believe that such wickedness lurks within these walls!"

"Wait," said Rama. "I have two more things to say.

"Firstly, I have spoken to my half-brother Bharata, and he had nothing to do with this business. He despises his mother for it, and swears that the throne shall remain empty until I return from exile.

"Secondly, my other brother Lakshmana knows of it too. He has offered to come with me when I'm banished into the forest. But what breaks my heart, dear Sita, is having to abandon you . . ."

"But Rama," the princess interrupted him, "you won't abandon me. I shall come with you too! What, do you think I'm afraid of wandering in the wilderness? What kind of weak soul do you take me for? When I married you, my love, it was to be with you for always. Come, so long as we are together, what more could we want for happiness?"

The old king died within the week, and with a heavy heart Bharata took up the reins of the kingdom and sent Prince Rama and his company away.

So Rama, Sita and Lakshmana set out for the depths of the forest. For many days they walked through ancient trees and thickets of creepers, followed by the flash of tigers' eyes and the sinister rustlings of snakes.

At last they came to a clearing watered by a crystal stream. Here they cut branches and vines and built themselves a rough hut, making it cosy with a little fire to cook on.

One evening they were sitting quietly chatting beside it, when Sita caught sight of a milk-white deer with huge, dark eyes leaping gracefully through the shadows.

"Oh, just look at that dear, pretty creature!" she cried. "If only I could look after it! Rama, can't you catch it for me?"

"You know your wish is my command," smiled Rama. "Let's see if I can get it." He stood up, then hesitated. "But Sita, I can't help worrying about your safety here. Promise that you'll keep close to Lakshmana all the time I'm away." He picked up a twig and ran around the princess, using it to scrape a rough circle in the ground. "And promise me too that you'll stay within this circle: may the gods grant it magic powers to protect and keep you safe!"

Sita nodded, laughing and, satisfied, Rama disappeared after the deer into the trees.

The other two waited, listening intently for a sight or sound of Rama's return. For a long time they heard nothing; until suddenly there came a distant cry:

"Help, help, come quickly!"

"It's Rama!" cried Sita. "He must be in some terrible trouble. Oh Lakshmana, you must hurry after him and see what has happened."

"But Sita," said her brother-in-law, "I'm meant to stay here and look after you."

"Don't be silly, I can look after myself. There's no time to waste – he might have been savaged by a wild beast or something. Please go after him, Lakshmana, – quickly."

So, uneasy as he was, Lakshmana did as she begged him.

All alone now in the little clearing, Sita paced anxiously up and down inside the magic circle that Rama had drawn around her. How still and eerie it was! But at last – yes, thank goodness – she heard footsteps hurrying through the trees.

A figure emerged into the clearing.

But it was not Rama, it was not Lakshmana.

Instead, a bent old man, thin and wasted, stood before her, holding out his begging bowl.

Sita gave a cry of sympathy at his bowed, emaciated body. Forgetting her promise and Rama's warnings, she jumped out of the magic circle, eager to give the poor old beggar a gift.

She held out some food, bowing her respects to the ancient man. But when she raised her eyes to look at him again, the beggar was not there. In his place stood a fearful demon!

He had ten heads and twenty arms, and his fiendish face was twisted with lust.

"Oh lovely lady," he hissed, "pretty Sita! While my enchanted deer lures your husband away I have come to rescue you from the forest. This is no life for a royal princess! But I, Ravana, King of the Demons, shall give you all the comforts and luxuries you deserve."

Before she could move, he grabbed her tightly. "Come and be *my* wife instead. Let us make each other happy at my home on the lovely island of Lanka!"

"Get off, leave me go!" Sita screamed at him. "Until the day I die, I shall never love any man except Rama!"

She pulled and pushed and pinched and even bit at him, but he had so many arms and such great strength that her efforts were less than nothing.

Then suddenly everything around her went black and she felt a sickening sensation of being whisked away through the air.

At Demon Ravana's palace on the isle of Lanka, evil lurked like poison in every corner, creeping up through the flagstones, fouling the water, turning the bird-song into moans and screeches, making the flowers wilt.

Every day, Sita waited for the hours to pass, chained to the high walls of a little garden. And every hour Ravana came to leer at her, with his ten ugly heads, prodding her rudely with a hundred clawed fingers, simpering, "Well my little jewel, have you changed your mind yet? Will you agree to be my wife?"

And every time Sita answered him, "Never, never! Through a hundred lifetimes, Prince Rama will be my only love!"

But one day while she was all alone there, a different voice came calling her:

"Princess Sita – is that you?"

She whirled round: there, crouching above her on the garden wall, was a huge monkey!

He jumped down and bowed graciously before her. "Greetings, I am Hanuman, king of the monkeys, son of the god of the wind. I have come to tell you that Prince Rama is mad with despair at your disappearance: he has done nothing but search since he discovered you were missing. He has asked me to help him find you."

From under his fur he pulled out a small golden ring. "He sends this as a token of his tender promise that he will rescue you very soon."

"Oh Hanuman, may all the gods shower you with blessings! Tell Rama my heart is in his keeping . . . "

Heavy footsteps came thudding towards the door outside the garden wall.

" . . . But quickly, the demon king is coming! Be gone while you can! Take . . . "

Before she could even finish, the monkey leaped safely out of sight. He was not a moment too soon, for just as his tail disappeared over the wall, Ravana strode in grinning horribly. "Sita, Sita, pretty little dabchick . . . "

Tight-lipped she sat, stone still, repelling his advances with greater courage than ever.

More days passed, slowly, slowly. Despite the promise of Hanuman's visit, nothing unusual seemed to happen.

Then one evening she heard distant whisperings from the demon guards who marched outside the garden walls:

"Lordy me, 'ave you seen what's 'appenin' to the sea? Someone's built a bridge right across it from the mainland!"

"Nah, nah, that's impossible. It's much too deep, much too wide."

"I tell you, it's true! a real bridge made of trees'n'boulders! Five days ago there was nothin', now it stretches all the way across. Who could . . . "

"Call to arms, call to arms! Will all demons fetch their weapons and assemble ready to fight immediately."

" 'Ey, what's goin' on?"

"There's a blimmin' great army of monkeys approachin' us, that's what!"

"Monkeys?"

"Yeah. No jokin' – they're armed to the teeth! King Ravana's got 'is war-cry up. 'N' you should see the geezer leadin' 'em – some prince, they say, but to me 'e looks more like a blimmin' god! Call to arms, call to . . ."

Sita's heart soared like a bird: it must be Rama, it *must* be!

Locked and chained in her garden prison, the gentle princess could do nothing but wait. Outside, the terrible sounds of battle shook ground and sea, while anguish exploded across the sky like a million raging fireworks.

For a hundred hours – no, a thousand days it seemed – she paced up and down in utter terror. Supposing dear Rama were wounded and dying? Oh, if only she could get out, to heal and comfort him! Supposing, despite faith and courage and Heaven's help, fearsome Ravana and his demon army should win?

By day screams and smoke blackened the sky; by night it was lit with evil flames and yellow demons' blood. On and on it went, forever waiting, forever dreading and longing . . .

Then at last a shriek that curdled her blood, turned her stomach to water, scarred ten times through the air.

(*Ten times for ten heads? If only – no, impossible, impossible . . !*)

As its last echo died, silence froze the world. Then there rose a babble of cracked and broken demon voices:

" 'E's got Ravana!"

"How?"

"In the heart with some kind of magic arrow . . . Bright as sunlight, it was!"

" 'Nah, nah, we're defeated!"

And now a terrible whining, wailing: "Our demon king is dead!"

Sita sank to the ground in sweet relief. Outside the garden wall, footsteps came hurrying. The door swung open and the princess leaped up:

"Oh my dear, sweet, brave Rama!"

Then words failed her in her happiness, though her face was radiant as new creation.

Rama came to her. Swiftly he freed her slender wrists and ankles from the cruel chains. She held out her arms to her husband, but he

did not respond. Their eyes met . . . and Sita's heart turned icy cold.

"Rama, don't stare at me like that! Whatever's wrong? Have you been wounded? Is it . . . ?

"Sita," said Rama in a choked voice, "I can't bear to look at you. To think . . . " he turned away and spat at the ground. "To think how that foul and horrible demon forced himself on you, and made you into his wife!"

"Oh, Rama," cried the princess, "why must you take my heart to be so weak? For all the force that Ravana used, I can swear by Heaven he did not in any way succeed!"

But it was as if Rama did not hear her. "How can I ever live with you again? All these times you've been held in that demon's arms will haunt our conversations and betray our every kiss."

"But, Rama, I beg you, listen to me. Though Ravana pleaded and threatened and terrified me hour after hour, I held him back utterly by the strength of my love for you!"

Rama threw her a glance that ached with pity and longing, but most of all with bitterness. "Don't make things worse with such lies! I'm afraid you're Ravana's widow now, Sita – not my wife."

Sita felt her knees go weak; her heart pounded and her eyes misted with tears. But she managed to keep her voice steady.

"Then why did you bother to rescue me, Rama?" she said quietly. "If that is really how you think of me after all this eternity that I've suffered and waited for you to come, I want nothing more than to die."

Her eyes fell upon Lakshmana, who waited motionless, expressionless behind his brother.

"Hey, brother-in-law," she called to him, "I beg you, come here and build a funeral pyre for me!"

Lakshmana's lips trembled.

"If that is what she wishes, you had better do as she asks you," Prince Rama said to him hoarsely.

So without a word, Lakshmana set to work and built a magnificent funeral pyre in the middle of that sorrowful garden. When it was ready, Sita climbed onto it, her face set, not glancing once at her husband.

The bitter flames were lit. They rose against the sky, engulfing Sita in a cloud of fire and smoke.

Rama turned away and his body shook. But suddenly Lakshmana gave a wild cry! "Brother, by Heaven, a miracle!"

Rama turned to look, just in time to see a great red vision rising from the heart of the fire, blazing like the sun.

"It is Agni himself!" he cried, falling to his knees. "Oh mighty god, Lord of Fire, what have I done that you should visit me?"

The god's voice crackled like lightning. "You have done your wife a cruel injustice, Rama. How could you let her kill herself like this? Do you not know and trust her after all this time? She has suffered the worst torments a woman can know, yet in all her deeds, her words, her innermost thoughts, she has always been utterly true to you."

The prince hung his head in shame and happiness as, gently, the god placed Sita into his arms.

"Now go and claim the kingdom that waits for you both," said Agni. "News of your imminent return has already reached the people and they are impatient to begin rejoicing."

Then, sudden as he had come, the fire god was swallowed up into the flames again.

So Rama took Sita by the hand and led her out of the garden with faithful Lakshmana at their side. They turned towards their kingdom. And on the wind, from thousands of miles away, they thought they heard their people calling:

"The demon is slain! Our king and queen are reunited and coming home! The spirit of the gods has come to rule on Earth!"

Why the Moon
Laughed

Ganesha — lord of literature, patron of merchants, remover of
obstacles — was feeling thoroughly fed up. It was all very well being
constantly told he was the most popular god in Heaven, but that
didn't make up for the way that everyone kept laughing at him.

All right, so he did have a fat, bulging belly — but what was wrong
with letting the Three Worlds see how much he enjoyed his food?

And it was true that he had nothing better than a raggedy old rat
to ride about on; but he couldn't help it, if that was all that he was
given.

And as for having to walk around with an elephant's head stuck
upon his shoulders . . .

"It's not my fault," sighed Ganesha to himself, "that Lord Shiva
cut my real head off." He was sitting in a quiet spot, feasting on the
offerings of food that some of his worshippers had just sent him.

"He never liked me, never wanted me, that was the real trouble."
He swallowed a couple of delicious milk-and-coconut sweetmeats to
cheer himself up. "Still, at least my mother loves me.

"It's not many who can truthfully claim goddess Parvati as their
mother! And me made pure and new from the dew of her body,
unadulterated by anything except a little handful of dust! No wonder
old Shiva was jealous. He could have been my father properly, of
course, but his mind was on other things at the time: wouldn't have
anything to do with the making of me. Well, that's his own hard luck.

"I don't know why he should start to grumble I was getting in his
way, though: how could I be, when my whole purpose in life is to
move things *out* of people's way?

87

"Anyway, I was only doing what I'd been told to by my mother. I can remember it quite well: 'No visitors today, please, Ganesha,' she said. 'Just you stand guard there at the gate, dear, and whatever happens, don't let anyone in.'

"Well, stand there I did, and who should happen along but mighty Lord Shiva. 'Stand clear,' said he, 'I want to see Parvati.' 'Oh no,' said I, 'not today Lord, the goddess has forbidden me to let anyone in.' 'Fool,' said Shiva (rather unkindly I thought), 'she doesn't mean to keep me out, I'm her husband, aren't I? Now just move yourself and let me enter.' 'No,' said I, for I love my mother dearly and always obey her – and the next thing I knew, Lord Shiva had lost that famous temper of his and sliced off my head!

"Oh, my mother was upset, I can tell you! So in the end, old Shiva had to give in and fit me on with a new one. Very kind and forgiving of him, I'm sure – but all the same, he could have got me something better than one he'd borrowed from an elephant!

"Still, got to keep cheerful. It certainly doesn't seem to stop my worshippers sending me the most tasty treats they can find! Mmm. these almond-and-honey things are nice!"

Ganesha looked down at the silver dish they had come on, but now it was quite empty.

"Ah well," he sighed, "time to be off, I suppose."

He stood up, swaying slightly with indigestion, and patted his belly contentedly. It was round and smooth, like a fine, ripe melon. He belched softly. Perhaps a bit of gentle exercise would do him good.

So he climbed carefully onto his rat. A quiet ride, jogging gently up and down in the pale moonlight – that's what he needed to help his meal go down. The animal settled into a comfortable trot and Ganesha leaned back, letting it lead him where it would through the beautiful, shifting shadows of the night.

But suddenly the rat skidded to a halt. Ganesha woke from his dreams and saw, stretched out across the path, a long, fat snake.

Cheeky thing! How dare it block the way that Lord Ganesha wanted to go?

"Come on Rat," the god urged cheerfully, "don't be scared. You'll just have to step over it, if it won't move."

He dug in his heels and the rat inched forward. Between his knees, Ganesha could feel the poor, scraggly creature silently trembling. It went very slowly, one step at a time.

"Eeeeh!" The rat stopped again with a high pitched squeal of alarm . . .

For the snake was rearing up, writhing and hissing, lashing its forked tongue at the rat. There was no time to shout a warning: with another shriek, the rat did a sudden about-turn combined with a double-somersault – and sent Ganesha flying!

For a few seconds he seemed suspended in the dark blue night air, while his rat fled and the snake waved its rudely hissing head . . .

. . . Then he was bouncing, front-ways-down, onto solid ground like a great rubber ball, with a thud-thud-thud . . .

. . . And *ow*!

Ganesha looked down at himself with a gasp of horror. The shock of bouncing had torn a great hole in his tightly stretched, over-fed belly!

Oh, the shame of it! How embarrassingly awful it looked. Whatever would everyone think and say now? He'd look more of a fool than ever – and all because of that stupid, arrogant snake.

"I'll make you pay for this, you nasty worm!" cried Ganesha, and he seized the snake, head in one hand, tail in the other, and wrapped it round and round his middle, until it had quite covered up the ugly, gaping hole.

"There, you stay put and don't dare move, you slithery, squirmy snake! Just you try and make up for the damage you've caused me."

Actually, when he looked down at it, Ganesha couldn't help thinking that the snake made quite a handsome belt. It certainly did a good job of holding his broken stomach in place.

"Hey, Rat," he called, "it's all right now. Danger's gone. Come on, let's be on our way."

The rat sidled up nervously. It sniffed at the ground, and then very suspiciously at the strange, gently breathing rope entwined around Ganesha's waist.

With a heave and a ho, Ganesha climbed back onto his raggedy steed and they rode slowly onward into the night.

Ah well, accidents happen, thought he to himself as he settled down comfortably again to his journey. The rat fell into its usual slow, rhythmic trot and Ganesha began to nod his way to sleep.

"Ha, ha, hah! Whatever's that stupid looking thing? Goodness, if it isn't Lord Ganesha! Trust the clumsy old elephant-head to go holding his middle up with silly pieces of string!"

Ganesha woke with a start and peered furiously around. If it wasn't one thing, it was another! Whoever was that now, daring to shower him with such insults? He couldn't see anyone, but still the insolent shouts of laughter rang noisily across the sky.

"Who's there?" cried the god, going hot and then cold with a new burst of rage. "Who's that, daring to mock me?"

"Oi, Elephant-face, it's me! No, I'm up here, you ninny!"

Ganesha looked up, following the direction of the voice; but all he could see was the Moon.

"Is that you, Moon?" he demanded.

"Yes, Ganesha, it's me! Oh, if only you could see yourself – what a sight! Split your tum from eating too much, have you? But what a way to try and patch it up . . . aah-hah-ha!"

"I'll teach you to laugh at me, you cheeky old planet!" cried Ganesha. "Here, take . . . take this!" And he wrenched one of the elephant tusks off his own head and flung it, like a discus, straight up into the Moon's face.

"Ha . . . ha . . . ha . . . *yow!*" The laughter suddenly turned into a pained yelp and then silence.

"Yes, I thought that would shut you up!" called Ganesha. "And you can have a curse to go with it as well, something that'll really hurt your pride, Moon. I'm going to make your light fade away every twenty-nine days – yes, fade away to nothing! How do you feel about that, eh? That'll teach you to poke fun at a harmless, well meaning god!"

"But, Ganesha," said the Moon in a small voice, "I've always heard you had a fine sense of humour. I didn't mean it unkindly, honestly. I thought you didn't mind a bit of fun about the way you look."

"There's fun and fun," said Ganesha shortly, "and lots of different ways of laughing. Take my worshippers now – they laugh with me, they know I'm one of them, and they cheer me up with flowers and sweets. But in your case, Moon, you were just being hurtful, mocking me when I've already got plenty of troubles. Don't you give a thought for my feelings?"

"I'm sorry," sniffed the Moon.

Ganesha shrugged. "So you ought to be! Well, just to make sure that you don't forget about it, I'm going to leave my curse with you forever. Yes Moon, every month until the end of Time, you'll be sorry for your unkindness when you have to lose your light!"

About These Stories

The stories in this book belong to a major living religion called Hinduism. Today Hinduism is followed by nearly six hundred million people, most of whom live in India and neighbouring countries, as well as in countries throughout the world where Indians have gone to live. Hinduism is said to be the world's oldest living religion. It had no single founder, but its roots are believed to go back at least 4,500 years.

Most Hindus believe that God is One and exists everywhere, throughout the universe, in every living thing. They feel that God is timeless, without beginning or end, without shape or form, neither male or female. But they also believe that God has many different faces, and often appears in the world, crystallised into clearly recognisable forms as the gods and goddesses of mythology.

There are two main faces or aspects of God in Hinduism. One is kindly Vishnu, who preserves and protects life. The opposite face is Shiva, who destroys life at the end of every Age. At first sight, Shiva seems to be rather severe and frightening, yet he is also full of goodness, for out of destruction he always recreates the universe again in a fresh and better form.

Vishnu and Shiva each have a wife, for Hindus say that God is female as well as male. Vishnu's wife is usually known as Lakshmi, and Shiva's wife is called Parvati, Sati, Uma, Durga or Kali. Shiva's wife is particularly important: indeed, in one of the myths she turns out to be more powerful than all the male gods put together. Although sometimes fierce and cruel, at others she is kind and motherly.

There are many other, less important gods and goddesses – so many that it can be rather confusing. Moreover, there are hundreds and hundreds of different myths about them, which have been collected and retold in the Hindu sacred scriptures over thousands of years. To help you get to know them, there is an alphabetical list below, describing the most important gods and goddesses who appear in this selection of popular stories. But remember, although each has a strong personality of his/her own, they are all really just different faces of the One God who lies behind them all.

GODS AND GODDESSES

The gods and goddesses live in Heaven, though they often come to Earth. In many ways they look and behave like humans – except that they do not blink, sweat or get dirty, and their feet never quite touch the ground; moreover, they have supernatural powers and can change their shape at will.

DEMONS

The demons, who come from the Underworld, sometimes also look like humans though they may be very deformed and ugly, or take on animal shapes. They too are masters of the supernatural and of magical changes. They generally represent the forces of evil; though in some myths they seem to be better behaved than the gods!

AGNI

The god of fire. He is red, with three legs and seven arms; his eyes and hair are black. Flames pour out of his mouth, and seven rays of light shine from his body. He rides a goat or a ram, and holds an axe, sticks of wood, bellows, a torch and a sacrificial spoon. His main role is to carry sacrifices from the priests to the gods, but he also burns demons.

BRAHMA

One of the most important gods. He is the Lord of Creation who made the universe, and is often known as 'the Grandfather'. He is wise and rather mysterious. His four heads each face a different corner of the Earth; and he also has four hands which hold the *Vedas* (the most sacred books of Hinduism). Sometimes he also carries a water-jug, a string of pearls, a dish or a sacrificial spoon. He rides on a goose, a swan or a peacock.

DURGA

A goddess, the form that Shiva's wife takes to destroy demons. She is very beautiful but also very fierce: she rides a lion and has ten arms, in each of which she holds a different weapon.

GANESHA

One of the most popular gods, loved and worshipped by numerous Hindus. His body is short and plump with a pot-belly, and he has the head of an elephant with three eyes and only one tusk. He has four arms and gives off a marvellous perfume which attracts bees, yet he rides a humble rat. He carries a writing pen with coloured inks, a rosary of beads, a spiked stick, a lotus flower and a tiger skin. His mother is the goddess Parvati. He is gentle, calm, sensible and friendly: as Lord of Obstacles, he removes all sorts of difficulties from his worshippers' way. His followers think of him with fond, amused affection, and always call on him for help before they go on a journey, move house, take an exam or even begin to worship another god, since to honour Ganesha is to guarantee success. He is the patron of literature, wisdom, good luck and prudence, particularly revered by writers and shop-keepers, and respected for his extensive knowledge and understanding of the holy scriptures.

HANUMAN

A monkey god. He is tall as a mountain, strong, agile and wise; his father is god of the wind, and thanks to this he can fly.

INDRA

'Lord of Heaven', 'Rider of the Clouds' or 'The Thunderer', is king of the gods and very important, though not as great as Shiva or Vishnu. He is god of rain, of storms, of fertility and of war; through the thunderclouds, he sends light and water to the Earth. He rides a white elephant or sometimes a chariot. He throws thunderbolts as weapons and also carries a bow and two lances. His home on Mount Meru, north of the Himalayas, is supposed to be the very centre of the Earth.

KRISHNA

One of the forms in which Vishnu was born on Earth to destroy evil. His mother was the cousin of a king who had killed all Krishna's brothers and sisters as soon as they were born, because it had been predicted that one of them would assassinate him; but Krishna's own life was saved as a tiny baby when his parents exchanged him for the baby daughter of a poor cow-herd. He was adopted and grew up humbly but happily amongst the cow-herds: their wives and children were particularly fond of him despite his terrible mischievousness. When he was older, he not only overcame demons, but also taught people on Earth a great deal of wisdom.

Modern Hindus still read about this in their holy book, the *Bhagavad Gita*.

LAKSHMI

The beautiful, golden, sweetly perfumed goddess of prosperity, and Vishnu's wife. She is usually shown sitting or standing on a white lotus blossom (a flower rather like a water-lily), while two elephants holding golden ewers sprinkle her with water from the holy River Ganges. Hindus particularly think of her at their festival of Diwali in October/November, when they place hundreds of tiny lights around their houses to welcome her and the good fortune that she brings.

PARVATI

Another beautiful goddess, one of the most important forms in which Shiva's wife appears. Pictures often show her sitting next to her beloved husband, talking earnestly about love or philosophy.

RAMA

A prince, one of the forms in which Vishnu was born on Earth. Many Hindus think of him as the 'perfect man' for he is brave, righteous, noble and devoted to duty.

SHIVA

One of the two greatest gods of Hinduism. He has three different forms. Sometimes he is a ragged holy man, practicing yoga and meditation. Then again he is shown as the bringer of fertility and new life, which is represented by a pillar called the *lingam*. Finally, he

95

may be pictured as Lord of the Dance, performing his cosmic dance within a circle of flames, and symbolising eternal movement, the wheel of life, all the joy and sorrow of the Universe. Shiva is mysterious and rather awesome; he is also quite difficult to understand, for he is full of opposites. He destroys life but also creates it; sometimes he seems almost mad yet he can also be gentle and kind; he often refuses to have anything to do with worldly pleasures, yet from time to time indulges in passionate love affairs. His skin looks very pale, for it is covered in white ashes, but he has a blue throat. His hair is often wild and matted, tangled with the moon or the holy river Ganges. He has a third eye in the middle of his forehead from which he can send out deadly flames. He wears a tiger-skin, has snakes twisted around his neck, his body and his arms, and often carries a skull or wears a string of skulls as an ornament. He rides a bull called Nandi. Frightening though he may seem, he is usually shown holding up one of his four hands in a gesture of reassurance.

SITA

A princess, one of the forms in which Vishnu's wife, the goddess Lakshmi, was born on Earth. Because of her gentleness, loyalty and loving devotion to her husband Rama, many Hindus think of her as the 'perfect woman'.

VISHNU

Together with Shiva, Vishnu is one of the two great gods of Hinduism. He is known as 'the Preserver', for he preserves and looks after the Universe and upholds goodness and righteousness. He has been born on Earth nine times in different forms: as a fish, a turtle, a boar, a half-man/half-lion, a dwarf, a man known as 'Rama-with-an-Axe', Prince Rama, Krishna and the Buddha (who founded the Buddhist religion). Each time he appears, his task is to even out the balance between good and evil – although he cannot ever totally destroy evil, since it is believed that good cannot exist without its opposite. It is said that he will be born on Earth once more – either as a rider on a white horse or as the white horse alone – when he will herald the end of the present Age. Vishnu has dark blue skin, and in his four hands he carries a club, a sea-shell, a discus-weapon and a lotus blossom. Around his neck he wears a sacred jewel. He rides Garuda, a creature that some say is an eagle, and others say is half-man/half-bird. He is often pictured sitting on a white lotus-blossom, next to his wife the goddess Lakshmi. His worshippers see him as very kindly and give him much love and devotion.

THE THREE WORLDS

In Hindu mythology, the Universe is made up of the Earth, the Air and the Heavens. Gods and demons move freely between the three.

AGES OF THE UNIVERSE

Most Hindus see Time as an eternal wheel, without beginning or end. But Time is divided into aeons, each of which consists of four Ages. The First is the Golden Age, when all creation is ruled by goodness. During the Second and Third Ages, evil gradually increases, until the Fourth or *Kali* Age which is full of disease and sin. It is said that at the present time we are living in a *Kali* Age. When at last the Universe has become so wicked that it cannot continue any longer, Shiva will destroy everything by fire and flood. But this will not really be the end. The Universe will sleep for a while and then everything will be made anew. All living things – plants, animals, people, gods and demons – will be created again and the cycle of four Ages will begin once more. Thus life and death, creation and destruction continue through all eternity.

Some Interesting Facts About Hinduism

WHAT DO HINDUS BELIEVE IN?

God. Most Hindus have their own favourite god or goddess whom they worship and pray to, hoping he or she will help them to reach the One, true God which lies beyond them all.

The soul. Most Hindus believe that every living creature has a soul.

Death and rebirth. Most Hindus believe that after death each person's soul is reborn again on Earth in a new body. This is called 'reincarnation'. Thus it is said that each of us has already lived hundreds of times before (although we cannot remember our previous lives) and probably will live hundreds of times again.

'Karma'. It is believed that good and bad deeds in our present life will determine the kind of life we will have next time we are born. Thus if you are honest and kind, next time you may be reincarnated into comfort and happiness; but if you are wicked, you may be reborn much lower down the scale – for example as a beggar or even as a monkey.

Enlightenment. Many Hindus feel that life on Earth is so full of suffering and sorrow that they would rather escape from the endless cycle of birth-death-rebirth. They believe it is possible to do this by reaching *moksha*, 'enlightenment', which means finding complete understanding of life and dwelling with God.

This is thought to be very, very difficult to do. Some Hindus try to achieve it by devoting their lives to worshipping their favourite god or goddess. Others seek enlightenment by filling their lives with good deeds. And some choose the 'Way of Knowledge', in which they use techniques such as yoga and meditation.

Respect for all life. Hindus believe that all living creatures deserve respect and kindness. They try to avoid doing violence to animals as well as to people, and some Hindus do not eat meat because they feel it is wrong to kill animals for food.

Truth has many forms. Most Hindus feel that Truth has many forms, that religion should have no single set of rules and that each person must find the path that is right for them in their search for God. Hindus accept a great variety of ideas and practices. Religions such as Christianity and Judaism are often accepted as different but equally valid ways of finding Truth.

HOW DO HINDUS PRAY?

A Hindu home has a corner set aside for worship, containing a picture or statue of the family's favourite god or goddess, often decorated with fresh flowers. Hindus usually say their prayers individually at home. Sometimes these might be just a few brief words murmured before the holy picture. On the other hand, very religious families have a regular ritual which they try to perform three times a day if possible. First they wash themselves carefully. Next they make an offering of flowers and food to the god or goddess, to say thank you for the good things in life. They may burn sweet smelling incense and a small oil-lamp, and use coloured powders to draw a beautiful sacred pattern on the floor, before meditating on God and saying their prayers.

There are countless temples and shrines throughout India and other Hindu areas, dedicated to different gods and goddesses. Some are small and very simple, others are huge and beautifully decorated with elaborate carvings, filled with the fragrance of incense and the chanting of priests. Hindus do not normally worship together as a congregation, but they may visit the temples at any time of day to make their offerings and to pray.

WHAT ARE THE HOLY BOOKS OF HINDUISM?

The holiest books are the four *Vedas* which contain sacred chants and hymns, prayers, rituals and the earliest myths and ideas about

God. They are very ancient: some parts are believed to be over three thousand years old. The *Ramayana*, a very long poem which contains the story of Rama and Sita, is about two thousand years old. Probably at about the same time another, even longer poem called the *Mahabharata* was composed: its three million words contain numerous myths and legends. The most famous part of it is the *Bhagavad Gita*, which some Hindus regard as their 'Bible'. Finally there are the *Puranas*, written between seventeen hundred and three hundred years ago, in which many other versions of the myths can be found.

Bibliography

O'FLAHERTY, W. (Ed.): *Hindu Myths: A sourcebook translated from the Sanskrit* (Penguin 1975)
JOHNSON, D. & J.: *God and Gods in Hundiusm* (Arnold – Heinemann 1972)
New Larousse Encyclopaedia of Mythology (Hamlyn 1968)
CAVENDISH, R. (Ed.): *Mythology – An Illustrated Encyclopaedia* (Orbis 1980)